GIRL
FORGOTTEN

OTHER MYSTERIES BY APRIL HENRY

Girl, Stolen
The Night She Disappeared
The Girl Who Was Supposed to Die
The Girl I Used to Be
Count All Her Bones
The Lonely Dead
Run, Hide, Fight Back
The Girl in the White Van
Playing with Fire
Eyes of the Forest
Two Truths and a Lie

THE POINT LAST SEEN SERIES

The Body in the Woods
Blood Will Tell

APRIL HENRY

GIRL
FORGOTTEN

Christy Ottaviano Books

LITTLE, BROWN AND COMPANY
New York   Boston

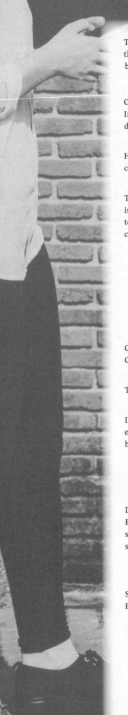

Christy Ottaviano Books
Hachette Book Group
1290 Avenue of the Americas,
New York, NY 10104
Visit us at LBYR.com

First Edition: March 2023

Christy Ottaviano Books is an imprint of Little, Brown and Company. The Christy Ottaviano Books name and logo are trademarks of Hachette Book Group, Inc.

The publisher is not responsible for websites (or their content) that are not owned by the publisher.

Little, Brown and Company books may be purchased in bulk for business, educational, or promotional use. For information, please contact your local bookseller or the Hachette Book Group Special Markets Department at special.markets@hbgusa.com.

Library of Congress Cataloging-in-Publication Data
Names: Henry, April, author.
Title: Girl forgotten / April Henry.
Description: First edition. | New York : Christy Ottaviano Books/Little, Brown and Company, 2023. | Audience: Ages 12+. | Summary: When seventeen-year-old Piper Gray starts a true crime podcast investigating a seventeen-year-old murder cold case, she puts her life in danger as she digs deep into the mysteries of the past.
Identifiers: LCCN 2022031746 | ISBN 9780316322591 (hardcover) | ISBN 9780316322850 (ebook)
Subjects: CYAC: Cold cases (Criminal investigation)—Fiction. | Podcasts—Fiction. | Mystery and detective stories. | LCGFT: Detective and mystery fiction. | Novels.
Classification: LCC PZ7.H39356 Gh 2023 | DDC [Fic]—dc23
LC record available at https://lccn.loc.gov/2022031746

ISBNs: 978-0-316-32259-1 (hardcover),
978-0-316-32285-0 (ebook)

Printed in the United States of America

LSC-C

Printing 1, 2022

For Aileen Woods Willes.
We went from girls to
women together. You were
always an early bloomer,
so of course you had to
run on ahead of me.
I miss you more than
you can know.

We appear to enjoy tragedy not despite,
but precisely because of, the painful
emotions we feel in response.
—S. Friend

The death, then, of a beautiful woman
is, unquestionably, the most poetical
topic in the world.
—Edgar Allan Poe

CHAPTER ONE

SAME AS ME
Sunday, August 23

MAYBE AFTER DARK, THIS older section of the cemetery, with its crumbling headstones, would be scary.

But it's a bright summer day, and right now, the cemetery is an escape. Peaceful, despite the busy road behind me. No little kids tearing around. No one asking me questions. No adults shooting one another looks when they think I won't see.

My mom would like this place. Which is a stupid thing to think. Like she'll ever see it.

Lost in memories, I stare at the raw brown earth of the new grave, a shocking contrast to the green surrounding it. A shout penetrates my earbuds. I've been listening to *Dead, Deader, Deadest,* my favorite true-crime podcast.

"Stop! Fred! Stop!"

I hit pause.

"Fred!"

I can't see the guy who's yelling, but he sounds frantic.

And barreling down the hill toward me, trailing a leash, is a golden retriever. Only a couple of feet in front of what must be Fred is a terrified squirrel. The two of them are going to run right past me. Hurtle into the busy street.

"Fred! Stop!" the guy yells again, his voice desperate.

I leap, my hand stretching out to grab the purple leash. My phone goes flying. It hits a headstone with a sickening *crack*.

The dog keeps going, almost jerking my arm out of the socket. Then, as the squirrel disappears under a bush, the dog stops and turns to face me, pink tongue lolling. He looks like he's enjoying himself.

At least one of us is.

When I pick up my phone, it's spiderwebbed with cracks. Tears sting my eyes, but on the other side of the hill, the guy is still shouting frantically for his dog.

Pulling Fred behind me, I start back in the direction he came from. After cresting a rise, I see a guy getting to his hands and knees. He's in the newer section of the cemetery, the one with flat metal plaques instead of headstones. He's about my age, with blue eyes and dark hair, wearing sweatpants and a rust-colored T-shirt.

"Oh, thank God." He brings his right knee up to put his foot on the ground. Then he raises his butt high in the air until he looks like he's trying to dive into the earth. With a groan, he awkwardly tries to pull his stiff left leg under him. But his balance fails him and he slumps back down to his hands and knees.

"You're hurt!" I start forward. Is it his ankle? His knee?

He raises one hand to keep me back. "I'm fine." He bites off the words. Fred strains toward him, but I tighten my grasp.

He tries again. Fails again. He's definitely hurt. Should I call 911?

"Could you help me?" he says reluctantly.

"Of course."

"If you put out your hands, I can use you to get to my feet."

"What about your dog?"

"Fred, sit."

To my surprise, the dog does, looking back and forth between us. I push my arm through the leash's loop until it's up to my biceps.

The guy crawls closer. I feel a little self-conscious about the length of my vintage denim skirt, with its deliberately ragged hem. I'm wearing it with a white T-shirt. For a belt, I threaded a red-and-blue scarf through the loops.

"Put one foot forward and bend your knees. Now give me your hands." He grabs them and I start to pull him up.

"Don't *yank* on me!" Red spots of color mark his cheeks.

"Okay, okay!"

"I'm sorry." His eyes shine with pain or embarrassment or maybe both. "I just need to steady myself on you. Don't pull and don't let go."

"Okay," I say again, but softer. Whatever's wrong, it's clear he can't bear a stranger witnessing it. I know how it feels to have people gawk at your pain. Stiffening my arms and legs, I make myself a statue. His grip grinds the bones in my hands together. I don't make a sound, just grit my teeth. He tries to swallow his groan, but I still hear it.

And finally he's on his feet, close enough that I can feel the heat of his body and smell his faintly spicy scent. He's about six inches taller than me, with a long nose and an upper lip that's a perfect cupid's bow. The skin above it is beaded with sweat.

We step back and drop our hands at the same time.

He doesn't meet my eye. When he holds out his hand, palm up, it takes me a second to realize he wants Fred's leash.

"Are you sure you're okay?"

"Yes." A flush creeps down his neck. I hand him the leash.

Without saying anything more, the guy turns and limps away. His left leg is stiff, his gait a bit like Frankenstein's monster. But at least his leg is still holding him up.

He doesn't even thank me.

Oh well. He's not my problem now.

I should go home. Home with quotes around it, I think.

Even though my dad and Gretchen say that's what I should call it.

Tomorrow's the first day of school, and I won't know a single person there. Unlike my mom, who stopped going to school when the morning sickness got too bad, Dad graduated high school. He went on to college and then law school.

Gretchen is Dad's current wife. Well, only wife, since he and Mom were never married. And by the way she presses her lips together whenever she looks at me, I'm guessing Gretchen worries I'm too much like my mom. A wave of loneliness crashes over me.

As I turn back, a spot of color catches my eye. A dozen pink roses wrapped in tissue and tied with a white satin ribbon lie on top of a marker. Next to the roses is an open bottle of Dos Equis.

I come closer to read the name and dates.

Layla Trello. She died seventeen years ago. And when she died, she was just seventeen.

The same age as me.

CHAPTER TWO

FOUL PLAY

Sunday, August 23

So what happened to Layla Trello? Cancer? Car accident?

Or—something squeezes my heart—maybe suicide? Was life just too much for her? The last few months have been an emotional roller coaster, so I can almost understand why someone might want to get off a similar ride.

As I start for home, I take out my phone to look her up. I forgot about the broken screen. One bottom corner is milky with cracks. My eyes spark with tears. My mom saved up for weeks to buy this off Craigslist. She'd worried it might be stolen, but the guy still had the original paperwork. He'd gotten a new phone and the old one was worth more on Craigslist than as a trade-in.

Even a year ago, this phone was out of date. Now it's ancient.

But it's still a connection to my mom. A connection I have literally broken. Because while I'm able to click out of the *Dead, Deader, Deadest* podcast, when I try to type *Layla Trello* into Google I have to jab some letters multiple times before they register.

While I don't regret grabbing Fred, couldn't his nameless owner have been a little more appreciative?

After waiting for a gap in traffic, I cross to the shadier side of the street. It's both cooler and easier to see the screen. At the top of the results are photos. Most are the same school portrait of a girl with dark blue eyes, long dark hair, and a spray of freckles across her nose. She smiles with closed lips. One photo shows her running, a number pinned to her chest. And one is a family portrait of two parents and two girls. Layla is the taller of the two.

Underneath the photos, the first link says, "Layla Trello Obituary on Legacy.com." Before clicking on it, I skim the links underneath.

"Hitchens Auto Dealerships Honor Layla Trello."

"Layla Trello—Girls' Track and Field Results."

"Layla Trello Memorial Scholarship Fund Established to Benefit..."

It's the bottom link that catches my eye. "Police Seek Public's Help in Finding Missing Teen Layla Trello."

I click.

(AP) Firview, Ore.—Police suspect a missing local teen may have met with foul play.

Firview Police Chief Benjamin Bassett says seventeen-year-old Layla Trello was last seen Friday night at a Halloween party. She left the party around two in the morning, but never arrived home.

Police want to speak to anyone who saw Trello that night.

I keep clicking and reading, clicking and reading, glancing up just enough to keep from tripping.

Nearly two weeks after Layla disappeared, her body was found in the forest six miles from here. She had been murdered. And as far as I can tell, her killer has never been caught.

CHAPTER THREE

EVIDENCE
Sunday, August 23

WHEN I WALK IN the door of the house that still doesn't feel like home, Gretchen is talking and no one is listening.

"I thought I bought Kleenex." She's pawing through the glue sticks, colored markers, folders, and crayons that cover the dining room table.

Gretchen's got big hands. Big everything. She's at least as tall as my dad, with broad shoulders. If her kids—Jasper and Sequoia—beg enough, she can carry both of them without effort, even though they're six and eight.

In the two months I've lived here, I've heard, more than once, how Gretchen has run the Boston Marathon three times. The first time while pregnant with Sequoia. The next year, pregnant with Jasper, with Sequoia in a stroller. The year after that, pushing a double stroller. It's not like my dad, Gary, wouldn't watch them. I think she just likes telling people she did it.

Ignoring Gretchen, Sequoia and Jasper are each holding the strap of a black backpack, pulling like it's a Thanksgiving turkey wishbone. On the table is a red backpack.

"I said I wanted the black one," Sequoia whines. She looks a lot like Gretchen.

"Nuh-uh," Jasper says. He looks more like my dad, with dark curly hair and blue eyes. "Mom said I could have it."

Sequoia yanks, making Jasper stumble forward. He loses his grip. Sequoia lands on her bottom and starts wailing, even though she now has the prize. Not to be outdone, Jasper's face scrunches up. But before he begins to cry, Gretchen says, "Stop it, you two! We'll just get another black backpack, all right?"

She pulls the backpack from Sequoia's grasp, her brown bobbed hair swinging. Her bangs end exactly at her eyebrows, and the rest is a sharp line that's even with her chin. Last week she eyed my messy blond bun, held in place with an old chopstick inlaid with pieces of abalone, and suggested she take me to her hairdresser.

I said no.

I've said no a lot to her.

Gretchen has never once complained about having to take me in. She doesn't have to. Her ice-blue eyes say more than words could.

Now those eyes focus on me. "What about you, Piper? Do you have everything you need?"

By high school, all the fun stuff has fallen off the list. No colored pens or folders printed with unicorns. But I have to tell her about my phone sometime. Might as well rip off the Band-Aid.

"Actually, the screen on my phone cracked. Could I borrow some money to get it fixed? I could babysit to pay you back."

Gretchen sighs. "First of all, you are a member of this family." She doesn't say the words with any warmth, but they still make me feel better. Then she adds, "So if you watch your brother and sister, that's something you do as a contributing family member, not because you expect to be paid for it like a stranger. And of course we'll pay for the phone. It looks old anyway. We'll just get you a new one."

She's had to introduce me a few times. *This is Gary's daughter, Piper.* Her lips will press together, like she's daring anyone to ask who my mom is or why I'm suddenly living with them. It's pretty clear her friends have never heard of me.

"I don't need a new phone." Sometimes it feels like Gretchen is keeping a running tally in her head, and I don't want to add to it. "Just getting the screen fixed will be fine."

While I'm speaking, my dad walks in the door.

"Gary, could you take your daughter to the Apple Store

and get her a new phone?" Gretchen says. "Her screen's cracked."

Your daughter. So much for being a family.

I interrupt. "I can just get the screen fixed."

Gretchen is a lawyer, same as my dad. Not like the ones that Kelley McBain talks to on *Dead, Deader, Deadest,* the kind who deal with murder. Gretchen is a tax attorney and my dad specializes in eminent domain law. He tried to explain it once—something about paying developers to take part of their property to build things like electrical substations—and I almost fell asleep.

Dad holds out his hand. "Let's see it."

I hand it over, glad I clicked off the Google search results for Layla Trello.

He winces at the cracks. "This is pretty old. It's amazing it's lasted as long as it has. What if we need to get hold of you or you get stranded someplace? You need a reliable phone."

The Apple Store is crowded, but thanks to his dark suit and ruby-red tie that shout "important businessman," Dad quickly attracts an employee with gauges the size of quarters. In less than ten minutes, Gauges has sold us a phone, earbuds, and a case, as well as gotten all my data transferred and put my SIM card in the new phone. He offers to recycle my old phone, but I say no.

My dad raises an eyebrow. "Might as well let it go."

I slip the phone into my pocket. "Maybe later." Even broken, it's still a link to my mom.

"Could her having both phones confuse the phone company?" Dad asks.

Gauges shakes his head. "Deactivated and without a SIM card, it can't make calls. Well, except to 911." He puts the lid back on the box for the new phone.

My dad holds up one finger. "I think we might need something else."

"What?" Gauges and I say simultaneously.

Dad turns to me. "You don't have a computer. You could use a laptop for school and at home."

The police kept the one I shared with my mom, saying they needed it for evidence.

I lower my voice. "Won't that cost a lot?"

Dad smiles and shrugs. "It's an investment in your education."

He and Gauges confer about memory and chips, and a few minutes later decide on a sleek silver laptop with lots of memory.

"You're probably going to want a dongle," Gauges says.

I blink. "What?"

"It lets you connect other things to your computer, like your phone."

We both look at my dad and he nods. Then Gauges disappears into the back to get everything.

"Thank you," I say, still stunned. Added all together, my dad has just spent the equivalent of two month's rent for our old apartment.

"Ready for school tomorrow?" he asks.

A pit opens in my stomach. "Yeah." I try to sound cheerful.

"I know all this has been hard for you." His soft tone almost breaks me. Luckily, Gauges appears with a bag.

As we're leaving, Dad gestures at the stores on the other side of the concourse. "Do you need new clothes for school?"

My plan had been to wear my thrifted mustard-yellow flared jeans and a short-sleeved cowboy shirt with snaps instead of buttons. At home with my mom, my real home, it was something I'd wear to school. But what will kids at North High be wearing?

"You've already spent too much," I say.

"Gretchen always gets the kids new clothes for back-to-school." Dad puts his hand on my shoulder. I tense, thinking he wants to hug me, but he just squeezes and releases. "Come on. Buy whatever you like. I'm sure tomorrow's going to be difficult. Might as well have some new clothes. Whenever Gretchen is facing a tough day, she wears this blue suit she calls her armor. Let's go get you your own armor."

CHAPTER FOUR

DID A KILLER WALK FREE?
Monday, August 24

THE NEXT MORNING, WHEN the alarm on my new phone rings, I resist the temptation to pull the covers over my head. I was up way too late reading about Layla Trello. Her case, which has never been solved, reminds me a lot of the ones on *Dead, Deader, Deadest*.

Before Gretchen wakes Sequoia and Jasper, I take a quick shower. Back in my room, I put on the new clothes my dad bought me last night. A pair of black jeans, a black shirt made of gauzy cotton, and some white sneakers with black soles.

People wear black to funerals. My dad told me that a hundred fifty years ago, mourners dressed from head to toe in black for a full year. In old movies, the bad guys wore black. Today, black feels like a blank slate, like I'm ready for anything.

Even breakfast.

Gretchen says we should "eat breakfast together as a family." In the time I've lived here that seems more like an aspiration than reality. Today, as usual, my dad is drinking coffee and reading the paper. He gets both the *Firview Times* and the *New York Times*.

I take my seat at the end of the table. Before I came, this family was a matching set of pairs: Gretchen across from Sequoia and my dad across from Jasper.

At the stove, Gretchen is heaping scrambled eggs in a blue serving dish. The air is fragrant with the salty smell of bacon overlaid with the sulfurous stench of slightly burned eggs. The red backpack over one shoulder, Jasper is racing around the dining room, Sequoia in hot pursuit.

"It's mine now!" he crows.

"It's not fair. I'm the oldest. I get first dibs." Sequoia stops and appeals to me. "And red goes with my outfit." She's wearing red leggings and a red-and-white-flowered dress.

Neither seems to remember that Gretchen went to the store last night so they could both have black backpacks.

"Actually, Sequoia, I guess you're no longer officially the oldest. Piper is." Gretchen plops some eggs on my plate. They have brown patches. She divides up the rest among plates. "Speaking of which, Piper, do you need a backpack?"

"I have one from last year."

She sets two pieces of bacon next to each pile of eggs. "Well, now you can have a new one." In one smooth motion she turns, catches Jasper, and pulls the backpack off his shoulder. "This is your sister's now. You two can have the black backpacks you wanted so badly yesterday. Now sit down and eat your breakfast."

She hands the backpack to me. Not knowing what else to do, I put it on my lap. Jasper and Sequoia sit, their angry eyes shooting daggers at me. Both of them mutter about the unfairness of it all, but in a volume designed to be deniable.

It's a relief to leave for school. Before I go, Dad presses a twenty-dollar bill in my hand "for lunch."

If Mom were here, she would take a picture of me in my first-day-of-school outfit while I rolled my eyes. Back then, I was so immature. Did she know then how much I loved her? Does she know how much I miss her?

North High is less than a mile away. Close enough to walk. It won't be fun once the weather gets cold, but today, when the temperature is going to end up in the eighties, it makes for a pleasant morning. The oak leaves are still a dark shiny green, the sky an untouched blue. Even so, there's a change in the air that lets you know fall is coming, with winter right behind it.

With the unfamiliar weight of the laptop inside my new red backpack thumping against my back, I begin listening to *Dead, Deader, Deadest*—known by fans as *Triple D*—and Kelley McBain's familiar low voice. I have to restart yesterday's episode because I lost the thread of the plot. In a lot of ways, it's always the same plot. An attractive girl or woman who is now dead, the usual suspects, a few surprises.

Last night I read that Layla also attended North High. Since she's buried only a few blocks from here, it shouldn't have been a surprise, but it still was. It made her more real.

I went to orientation last week, feeling hulking among all the ninth graders. When had they gotten so small? I seemed to be the only transfer student. After getting my schedule and books, I was assigned a locker. Later a senior girl gave us a tour, and explained lunch and passing time.

I turn on the street leading to the school. Students climb out of a stream of cars. More get off yellow buses. In my ears, Kelley McBain says urgently, "Was the wrong man charged? Did a killer walk free? And was important evidence completely overlooked?"

With each step, I fight the urge to turn around. I can't get back to my old life. All I can do is move forward. I switch off the podcast and follow the hordes inside.

CHAPTER FIVE

PASSION PROJECT
Monday, August 24

In only a few minutes, I'm lost. The school's layout made sense when it was empty, but not so much when filled with buzzing students. As the halls clear out, anxiety tightens my throat. When the bell rings, the last few people go sprinting. By the time I finally figure out which hall holds the writing classes, the only people in it are me and a guy coming from the opposite direction. He's walking with a strange, hitching gait.

It's the guy from the cemetery. Fred's owner.

"You *were* hurt!" I blurt out.

Putting his finger to his lips, he opens the door. As the last ones in, we both end up in the front row, sitting next to each other.

"Welcome, welcome!" the teacher says. Wearing a turquoise top that sets off her shoulder-length blond hair, she extends a box of Krispy Kremes toward us. Only two are left. The rest are being eaten by my classmates. I take one.

The guy hesitates. "But what about you, Mrs. Wharton?"

I stop mine an inch from my watering mouth.

She smiles. "No worries, Jonas, I ate one before class started."

I bite down, my mouth flooding with water, as Jonas takes the last one.

After setting the box down, our teacher hooks her hair behind her ears. "This is Creative Writing and I'm Virginia Wharton. So if this isn't where you should be or you've come to your senses, now's your chance to escape." She pauses as if someone might actually leap up. "Okay, the first thing I want you to work on while I take attendance is to use all five senses to describe your doughnut—without using the words *doughnut* or *Krispy Kreme*."

Opening my new laptop, I start writing about the doughnut's yeasty smell and the way it yields to my touch. She begins calling roll. At my name, I look up and answer, "Here."

Her bright blue gaze regards me. "You're new this year, aren't you, Piper?"

"Yes, ma'am. I moved here from Eugene."

"Well, welcome."

The guy's full name is Jonas Shortridge. He seems to be making a point of not looking at me, so I make a point of not looking back.

Mrs. Wharton says, "This year, one thing we'll be working on is showing, not telling. If you wrote that the doughnut is tasty, that's telling. I want to feel like I'm the person eating the doughnut. So for the next exercise, write about it again, only this time imagine it's being eaten by a famous person or your favorite character. Write five or six sentences in first or third person showing this individual eating it. While you can use the word *doughnut*, you can't use any form of the word *be*: *am, is, are, was, were, be, being, been*. Those are words that lead to telling."

How would Kelley McBain regard my two-thirds-eaten doughnut? Probably as a clue. I write about the shape of the tooth marks, the fact that it still seems fresh, and the lack of smudges on the spongy white interior, indicating that whoever held it had clean hands.

Next Mrs. Wharton says, "Write about the doughnut again, only this time don't use adverbs or adjectives. A word that ends in *ly* is just calling out for a stronger verb." As she goes through first-day busywork, like checking out Chromebooks to those who need them, Mrs. Wharton keeps giving us new exercises for the by-now-long-departed doughnuts.

It's actually fun.

One by one, we are sent down the hall for school pictures. I feel a pang for my old self, the kid who wanted the picture package but whose mom usually didn't have the money to pay for it. The portable background screen is a weird blotchy blue, like the one in Layla's photo. Maybe it's even the same one. I smile and hope it doesn't come across as fake as it feels.

By the time class ends, I've relaxed a little. The rest of my classes are more formal. Unfortunately none of them involve doughnuts. I mostly feel invisible, but I don't mind. It gives me a chance to figure things out. The only tough time is lunch. It's easy to tell which tables hold the popular people, the jocks, or the theater kids. In my old school, I wasn't part of any of those groups, but I still had friends. I scan the room but don't see Jonas. I take a seat at a table with several empty spots, thankful I have my phone for company. I put on my earbuds and listen to the rest of the *Dead, Deader, Deadest* episode while eating tacos.

At the end of the day, the seniors are called out for an all-grade assembly. As we file in, the cheerleaders, dressed in blue and gold, are doing a tumbling routine. I spot Jonas on the other side of the auditorium.

Principal Barry, a wiry, nervous man, gives us a quick rundown of school values, including respect for authority and ourselves. That means everything from not letting others copy to no crop tops.

Has he ever looked at the cheerleaders' outfits?

He's followed by Officer Balboa, the drug liaison officer. He peppers his "Just say no" talk with slang that was popular back in elementary school.

After him, a blur of adults are introduced: the guidance counselors, the nurse, the librarian, and the yearbook advisor. That's Mrs. Nelson, who looks older than God, and who wears turquoise reading glasses on a pink lanyard. She encourages people to submit photos for the yearbook. "Now that everyone has a camera in their hand, you can all help tell the story of this year."

Principal Barry takes the mic again. "Of course, the highlight for most of you will be your senior passion project. These allow you to explore something that interests you via experiential learning throughout the entire year."

At my old school, we didn't have a senior passion project. In fact, it was pretty much expected that most of us weren't that passionate about school. Plus a senior passion project sounds like a lot of work.

Principal Barry starts tossing out possibilities. Create a graphic novel. Or volunteer in a local official's office. Film a documentary. Build and stock a Little Free Library or a Little Free Pantry. Help out at a retirement home. Intern for the local paper. Start a community garden. Coach a Special Olympics team.

It all seems overwhelming. What am I even passionate about?

"The first step will be proposing your project to your advisor."

Then I remember *Dead, Deader, Deadest*. Everyone knows Kelley McBain got her start podcasting in her bedroom. Now she has hundreds of thousands of listeners.

I'm already getting excited. A podcast! And I know just whose story to cover.

Layla Trello's.

CHAPTER SIX

BE WHOEVER YOU WANT
Monday, August 24

ON MY WALK HOME, I call Chloe. I actually have to look up her number. I can't remember if it ends in six-two or two-six. Usually I'd be able to find her in my recent calls, but I haven't talked to her for . . . I'm not sure how long.

I'd worried she was forgetting me. But maybe I'm forgetting her.

"Hey," Chloe answers.

"It's me." Then I add, "Piper," in case there's another "me" in her life now.

Which is silly. Chloe and I have been best friends since third grade. Just because I now live a few hours away doesn't change that. The only reason we've been texting and talking less is we've both been busy. It's no different from the year her grandma paid for her to go to camp, where she had the kind of summer kids in books always did, swimming in a lake and sleeping in a cabin filled with bunk beds.

"So what was the first day of school like without me?" The sun is a warm hand on my back. I put a fingernail between my teeth, then snatch it out. Nibbling my nails is a bad habit I want to break.

I wait for Chloe to say, "Everybody asked where you were." But instead she starts talking about who dyed their hair, who's gotten muscles, whose social media blew up, and this one girl who got pregnant.

I find myself having a hard time conjuring all these people in my mind's eye. This summer, a few kids from school stopped by the Over Easy. They ordered lattes to wake themselves up, or French toast to absorb the alcohol still sloshing around in their systems. But most of our regulars were truckers and older folks who had no interest in lattes, just coffee poured from a pot. They came in for the four-egg omelets, the hash browns, and the pie.

On the bus home from work, dressed in our matching white polos and pink skirts, my mom and I used to have fun discussing the customers. The memory makes me blink back tears.

"Did anybody ask about me?" I finally ask Chloe as I unlock the door to an empty house.

My dad and Gretchen are at work, the kids at their after-school program. I'd been worried I might be expected to babysit. But it seemed I was the only one who thought about how much money they could save by canceling my half-sibs' "enrichment" program, a continuation of a summer that's been filled with day camps featuring archery, pottery, painting, and horseback riding.

"Oh, a lot of people did," Chloe says, but I can hear she's not telling the truth. It's like everyone's forgetting me. Including me. "Besides, why care about them? At your new school you can be whoever you want. You can be the pretty one, the popular one, the partier."

"All those options sound kind of shallow," I object, heading for the kitchen.

"Okay, then be the unique one. The artist. The Mathlete. Although it's probably too late to be a band geek."

"Especially since I don't play an instrument." We both laugh, thinking about the recorders we all got in third grade, the closest to band or orchestra our low-income elementary school got. We drove our moms insane with our constant tootling.

"Is your new school much different?" she asks.

I take a slice of processed cheese from the fridge. Since Gretchen bought it, the label claims it's organic, colored with carrots, and made with non-GMO milk. "They have a lot more electives. I guess the parents fundraise for them. Some cars in the student parking lot are nicer than the teachers' cars." I unwrap the plastic, fold the slice in half, and take a bite. "And Dad and Gretchen have so much money. They spend it without thinking about it. It's obscene considering how my mom had to live."

Chloe says, "But when your dad used to come visit, didn't you say he always wanted to buy you things, but your mom told you to say no?"

Sometimes there are downsides to having been friends for so long.

After taking another cheese square, I use my hip to close the fridge door. "Yeah, but it was important to my mom that he didn't think of us as poor. But don't worry, I'm making up for lost time. He bought me a new iPhone. And while we were in the Apple Store, he insisted I get a new laptop." I devour the second slice of cheese.

"Whoa! Sweet!" There's not a trace of jealousy in Chloe's voice.

"It'll be useful for the one thing that's definitely different at this school. We have to do a senior passion project that lasts the whole year." I bury the cheese wrappers in the stainless steel garbage can.

"What are you going to do?" Chloe asks.

"I'm going to make a podcast like *Dead, Deader, Deadest* about this old unsolved murder. A girl our age who died seventeen years ago." I sketch out who Layla was and what happened to her. As I do, a prickle runs down my spine. Her story fascinates me. It's exactly like something Kelley McBain would talk about.

But in the middle of detailing how Layla was murdered,

I realize Chloe's murmurs of agreement have dropped to almost nothing. I interrupt myself.

"I forgot to ask—did I call at a bad time?"

"Not really. It's just that right now I'm actually hanging out with Redmond."

"Redmond? Redmond Strickland?" Redmond is at least three inches shorter than Chloe.

"He grew like five inches this summer. We've kind of been spending time together lately."

It's like she punched me in the stomach. Her getting a boyfriend is a big deal, but she didn't think I was important enough to tell. When I say maybe I should go, Chloe doesn't even argue.

I put my phone in my pocket, pushing away thoughts of our distance. Instead I think about Chloe's advice. At North, I *can* be whatever I want to be. I don't have to be "That poor girl, did you hear about her mom?"

I can be the girl who has her own podcast.

CHAPTER SEVEN

TRAUMATIC LIFE CHANGE
Monday, August 24

A<small>FTER TALKING TO</small> C<small>HLOE</small>, I walk through the house. Gretchen—or maybe my dad or both of them—picked soothing, neutral colors. The furniture is sturdy, oak and leather. The art on the walls is mostly photographs. One shows a line of colorful doors along an Italian cobblestone street. Another is a close-up of what Gretchen told me was the bark of a Hawaiian rainbow eucalyptus tree. Its peeling vertical layers are electric green, orange, red, teal, purple, and blue. It looks like an abstract art project.

And these aren't just prints bought at a gallery. They're places they've actually been. Photos they took themselves. Meanwhile, the only vacations my mom and I took were to the coast, a two-hour drive away.

My mouth twists as I pass a photo of a huge moon

rising over white buildings in a Greek beach town. It doesn't seem fair, even though my mom always harped on how she had showed everyone that she could stand on her own two feet, of how she had made something of herself when no one else thought she would.

At least she had until the very end.

I go upstairs to what still doesn't feel like my room. Sprawled on the bed—which Gretchen insists be made every morning—I listen to more *Dead, Deader, Deadest*, but with completely different ears. It must be like how an architect looks at a building and sees the structure's details. How does Kelley shape the story? How does she present the twists? What order does she tell it in? I take notes on my new laptop.

She always starts with the crime. That's the hook. Then she moves back in time to talk about the victim. After that, she discusses various suspects. Toward the end, Kelley touches on some possibly related crimes as well as various theories about what happened. Along the way she interviews friends, enemies, and law enforcement. But she's Kelley McBain, and I'm just me, a high school student. Who will even want to talk to me?

When the episode is over, I watch videos about podcasting. Some are confusing, full of unfamiliar terms. Some are daunting, talking about expensive microphones and mixers. But then I find one where a college girl talks about how you can start with what you have, even if it's just a laptop and earbuds. She mentions a program called GarageBand, which actually came loaded on my computer. Maybe I can do this.

Two days later, I meet with my advisor. Ms. Kernow has red hair and so many freckles it looks like someone spattered her with paint. Even though school's just started, every available flat surface in her office is already covered with stacks of papers and file folders. She leans on her desk while I take one of the two visitor chairs.

"First of all, I want you to know that I'm always available to talk, Piper. Since you're a transfer student, I wanted to meet with you right away, as it can be a little hard finding your footing in an unfamiliar location. I myself only started here this year. And I also understand you've recently suffered a traumatic life change."

Traumatic life change. I guess that's one way to put it. I don't want to talk about my mom with a stranger. Someone who doesn't know me and will never know her. Someone who is paid to pretend to care. And even if Ms. Kernow really does, it's still too raw and strange.

"Okay," I mutter, looking down at my lap. I'm wearing a blue plaid pinafore dress with a white short-sleeved blouse. The dress looks like a Catholic schoolgirl uniform, and might actually have been one before it ended up at a thrift store. To contrast with the primness, I'm wearing black Doc Martens.

I'm relieved when Ms. Kernow returns to talking about school. "Now, here at North, as Principal Barry said, you'll be working on a senior passion project the whole year. Senior projects always look great on transcripts, so you should choose something that could appeal to the college you want to attend." She interrupts herself. "Oh, I just need to make a note for your file. Where do you want to go?"

"Maybe a community college?"

"According to your transcript, your grades are excellent. You should think about setting your sights a little higher." She blows air through pursed lips. "Let's revisit this later. So do you have any ideas for your passion project?"

"I want to do a podcast."

Her eyes get a fraction wider and she nods appreciatively. "On what? Politics? Humor? Fashion?"

I hold her gaze and simply respond, "Murder."

CHAPTER EIGHT

JUST FLIP A SWITCH
Thursday, August 27

I T TURNED OUT Ms. Kernow is a fan of *Dead, Deader, Deadest*, so she had no problems with the topic. Instead she wanted to know how I'll learn to podcast.

After I said with YouTube and books, she suggested a possible mentor. Not a teacher, but another student.

"His name is Jonas Shortridge."

"Oh." Fred's owner. The guy from Creative Writing.

"He started his late last spring. He had to find a new way to participate in sports after his, um, accident."

Accident? Ms. Kernow looked so uncomfortable I didn't ask for details. Whatever it was, it was big enough that she assumed I knew the story. Maybe Jonas's limp was not just Fred's fault.

"I'll arrange for you two to meet during free period tomorrow."

We haven't exchanged one word since the day we met. He doesn't ever meet my eye in Creative Writing. Then again, he doesn't meet anyone's eyes.

The next day, though, Jonas leans over before class starts. "Ms. Kernow says I'm supposed to give you some advice on starting a podcast. Want to meet in the library during free period?"

"Sure," I say as Mrs. Wharton moves to the front of the room. She starts explaining point of view. Third person can be as close as a thought or as impersonal as a camera. How close do I want to get to Layla's story?

A couple of hours later, I find Jonas settling in at a table at the very back of the library. The table closest to us has a backpack and a pile of books, but no person.

"How's Fred doing?"

"Fine. I don't think he'd know what to do with a squirrel if he actually caught one. He's not a big thinker. I appreciate you stopping him."

Ms. Kernow's words echo in my head. *After his accident.* "*Were* you hurt when you fell?"

"Just my pride."

The limp must be from his accident. It's probably the reason Fred was able to get away in the first place.

"You just transferred here, right?" Jonas asks.

It's like we're both inadvertently going for each other's weak spot.

"Yeah." After unzipping my backpack, I take out my new laptop. "I was living with my mom, but I had to move in with my dad a couple of months ago."

Jonas hesitates, then asks, "What happened to your mom?"

"She's dead." I say it fast and flat, like it doesn't bother me at all. But I don't meet his eyes.

I remember the day my whole world turned upside down. When I walked into our apartment after school, all the drawers and doors stood open, the contents jumbled. Too scared to call my mom's name, I kept moving. The kitchen sink was filled with dry cereal, the empty boxes lined up on the counter. Someone had clearly been looking for something.

And then I had opened her bedroom door.

Jonas sucks in a breath. "Oh my God, I'm sorry."

"That's okay." I make myself think of my podcast, not my mom. "Anyway, I appreciate you meeting with me to explain how to get started podcasting."

He rubs his left knee. "Ms. Kernow said peer-to-peer mentoring will look good on my college application."

I make a face at how stilted he sounds. He turns and catches it before I can smooth it out. His eyes narrow.

A faint shout brings our attention to the nearest window, which is open a few inches. A PE class is running on the track. They don't seem very enthusiastic. Layla would have left them all in the dust. When I turn back, Jonas is watching them with his teeth sunk into his lower lip.

"Ms. Kernow said you started your podcast last spring?"

"Yeah." He gives his head a shake as if trying to make his brain change the subject. "I learned a lot the hard way. It's not like you can just flip a switch and have your podcast magically appear on everyone's phones. It takes way more time than you think. For every hour of airtime, I put in at least seven hours. Picking the topic, researching, finding someone to interview, writing the questions, recording, editing, doing the voice-over, and then putting it all together. There's a ton of work before you even upload your first episode."

As he speaks, I start taking notes. Ms. Kernow said a passion project requires a minimum of eighty hours. Sounds like I'll have no trouble making that.

"You need to think about your target listener," Jonas continues. "How old are they? What kind of job do they have? What are they interested in? What TV shows do they watch? And most important, what other podcasts do they listen to?"

I figure all I need to do is ask myself those questions.

Jonas tilts his head. He's more relaxed now that the subject is podcasts. "How often are you going to put it out? Daily? Weekly? Monthly? Once you promise a cadence, you need to stick to it."

"I was thinking weekly." That's what Kelley McBain does. Of course, she covers a whole crime every week, and I'll just be putting Layla's story up in pieces.

He nods. "You should post at least two episodes the first time. That hooks listeners by giving them something to binge. And keep in mind that people listen to podcasts for the same reasons they listen to books on tape."

"Because they're interested in the topic," I say.

"That, but also because they want to listen while they do something else, like running or cleaning. For most people, it's commuting. A lot of weekly podcasters post on Friday, but I think that's a mistake. I post on Sunday night to catch all those commuters."

"Okay." I'm barely keeping up.

"And remember that a podcast isn't like YouTube. There are no interesting images that can make up for poor sound. All you have are people's ears, so the sound quality needs to be good. You should get a decent mic. And you should record in a small room. Some people even record in a blanket fort."

"A blanket fort?" I echo. The words bring back little-kid memories of pulling up chairs next to the couch and stretching a blanket over everything. I loved that. I felt so safe. Like a bear in a cave. Suddenly, my heart is a weight.

"If you're in a bigger space, the words might echo."

I nod and keep typing.

Jonas offers me what is almost a smile, and it transforms

his face. "Now if you're a perfectionist like me, you'll never like the way you sound, or you'll want to keep looking for the absolute best way to frame things. But done is better than perfect. You don't want to have perfection paralysis."

This close, I notice a faint white scar in his hairline, just above his temple. Does it have anything to do with the mysterious accident?

"You're going to need to set up your podcast host account. The host account will give you the feed for the RSS—that stands for really simple syndication—and publish it to podcast players."

By this point, I'm just trying to type everything in without understanding ninety percent of it. Jonas puts his hand between my eyes and the keyboard, forcing me to stop.

"Look, I'm sorry, this is turning into a big info dump. Maybe I should just give you assignments one at a time."

"Okay." I sit back and roll my shoulders.

He taps a finger against his lips, thinking, then points at me. "How about this. Your assignment, should you choose to accept it, is to think of a title and then make a logo for it—that little thumbnail people see when they scroll through podcasts. There's literally more than a million podcasts on Apple, so you don't want to do anything that hurts your chances of being noticed. First, make sure no one is already using your title. You want one with good searchability. Definitely no weird spellings. Something that lets a potential listener know what your show is about."

I lean forward. "Oh, I already know what I'm going to call it. *Who Killed Layla Trello?* The title will make it clear it's about a true crime. Layla was actually a student here when she was murdered seventeen years ago."

"Great." Jonas's voice is flat. He crosses his arms.

I take a deep breath for courage. "Is something wrong?"

"It's just our podcasts don't have anything in common. I cover the best games in various sports. You, on the other hand, want to bring attention to someone's worst moment."

I cross my arms. "Bringing attention to the case might get it reopened. Some of the cases that the podcast *Dead, Deader, Deadest* covers have been solved after the episode aired."

As I'm speaking, the owner of the abandoned backpack appears. It's a girl with shiny black shoulder-length hair, parted in the center.

"Hey, Alice." Jonas's voice completely changes. Now it's soft, hesitant.

She doesn't answer. Her dark eyes don't even look in our direction. Her silence is as strong as a shout. She puts her books into her backpack and slings it over one shoulder. It's like the two of us don't exist.

Alice's departure leaves a space like a vacuum.

"She used to be a friend of mine," Jonas finally says.

I can fill in the blanks. A girlfriend. And it didn't end well.

CHAPTER NINE

UPSIDE-DOWN WORLD
Thursday, August 27

THE FIRST THING I do when I get home is order the cheapest of the microphones Jonas showed me. I'm allowed to use the family's Amazon account. Even the kids are. Every day a pile of brown boxes and white padded envelopes sprawls on the porch.

Next I work on the logo using the free website Jonas suggested. The website doesn't explicitly have templates for podcast logos, so I scroll through the premade logos for imaginary bakeries, lawyers, and car repair shops. I pick one that says "Blaze Baller," with *Blaze* in white and *Baller* in aqua. I like the stylized letters. All the crossbars, like on the *B* and the *E*, are on a slant.

I replace *Blaze* with *Who Killed* and *Baller* with *Layla Trello?* I'm not sure about the aqua, but when I change it to red, it's too harsh. After trying other colors, I end up going back to aqua.

On Creative Commons, I find a royalty-free photo of an old blank tombstone to layer under the words. I wonder why it never got used. The tombstone, I mean, not the picture.

When I drop the photo in the background it's a little crooked, so I google how to rotate it a few degrees. The whole thing looks great.

I think I'm done, but then I check my notes. Even though the logo I just created is square, like it's supposed to be, it's not the right number of pixels. I have to start over, but everything goes faster now that I know what I want.

I'm just centering the words on top of the tombstone when Gretchen knocks lightly on my door.

"Piper? Time for dinner."

Belatedly, I realize she's said my name more than once. "Sorry!" I leave my room and follow her downstairs. "I kind of got lost in my homework."

She nods in approval, setting her hair swinging and exposing the pale nape of her neck. "Let's hope that attitude rubs off on your brother and sister."

The words remind me of the strange, upside-down world I now live in. Until this summer, I'd only seen Jasper and Sequoia a handful of times. Now I live with them. Now they're my family.

At dinner, the kids vie for their parents' attention. When my dad dutifully asks me about school, I just say I have a lot of homework. Gary and Gretchen seem like the kind of parents who might want to have a say in my choice for the senior passion project, and my gut tells me they wouldn't approve. The first week I moved in, Gretchen asked me what I was listening to. When I said *Dead, Deader, Deadest*, she frowned. But tonight no one presses me for details.

"And he's a bunny and his name is Firecracker and someone gets to take him every weekend and I think it should be us," Jasper says in a single breath.

At the same time, Sequoia is narrating every step of her day. "At lunch I traded it for a Fruit Roll-Up. But it was grape flavored." She makes a face.

Meanwhile, Gretchen says something about briefs that need to be filed, and my dad is saying his car needs to go in for service. It's like there are four competing conversations going on.

Back in my room, I take another look at the logo. It looks strong and bold. If I saw it pop up as a new podcast, I would definitely click on it.

It helps that Layla Trello is a cool name. *Layla*, like that old song. And *Trello* sounds Italian. It doesn't seem fair that if her name was something like Jennifer Smith, fewer people might click.

Although who am I kidding? Everyone knows certain

groups of people get more attention if something bad happens. Pretty, young white women. If they're blond, even better. It helps if they can be shortened to "Missing Teen" or "Murdered Mom." Nobody cares as much about "Missing Man" or "Murdered Old Lady."

Even though the logo feels like a big step, I've barely scratched the surface of what needs to be done. I also have to figure out how to cover the story. It makes sense to follow in Kelley McBain's footsteps and devote the first episode to the crime. I've found several articles online. Not just in the *Firview Times*, but a couple in the *Oregonian* and one each in the *Washington Post* and the *New York Times*. I can combine and rewrite what they covered.

But how can I make it as good as *Dead, Deader, Deadest*?

CHAPTER TEN

PRIME SUSPECT

Saturday, August 29

WHERE DO YOU GO when you want to learn things? Or at least where would you have gone when Layla was still alive?

No, not the internet. The public library. I've done all the googling I can think of, but there must be more information out there.

I haven't been to a library since I was in grade school. Sometimes when my mom was desperate for a babysitter, she would drop me off there, a place both safe and free.

On Saturday morning, I take a bus to Firview's public library, which to my eye looks more like a courthouse. I walk up the shallow stone steps, worn down in the middle, and under the portico held up by two stone pillars.

Inside is one big open room with tall narrow windows

and high ceilings. In the back, dozens of newspapers hang on wooden rods. The old issues must be underneath. But when I check the shelves, I find only issues from the past few months. Certainly nothing seventeen years old.

I venture to the information desk. Sitting behind it is a woman with wire-rimmed glasses and short curly brown hair. Her name tag reads KAREN. She smiles.

"I'm looking for information about something that happened seventeen years ago." When I add, "A murder," her eyebrows rise. I tell her Layla's name and my podcast idea while watching her expression. Will she, like Jonas, think I'm ghoulish?

"I moved here about ten years ago, so I don't think I've ever heard of the case." Karen tilts her head. "But it sounds fascinating."

"I thought I might find more information in old newspapers." I point at the section. "But those aren't old enough."

"Our older issues are on microfiche to save space."

A microfiche, it turns out, is a flat piece of film holding microphotographs of a publication's pages. As Karen locates the microfiche for the *Firview Times*, she asks, "And they never caught the killer?"

"No. But maybe the podcast will shake something loose."

She demonstrates how to pull the machine's handle until the glass pops up, slide the microfiche under the glass, and then push the handle back into place to display the image on the screen. "Then move the tray around until you find something. Are you going to want printouts?" When I nod, she says, "I'll trade you your ID for a print card. Put it in this slot and then press this button to print."

The first three articles I find I've already read. I keep scrolling.

TRELLO MURDER INVESTIGATION CONTINUES AS FRIENDS SPEAK OUT

Firview, Ore.—Police have identified the body found in the woods last week as seventeen-year-old Layla Trello, who has been missing for nearly two weeks. Trello was discovered on Wednesday by a person gathering bear grass in an area known as Bettinger Butte. She was last seen at a party on Halloween night in North Firview. An autopsy showed she died of a single gunshot wound to the heart.

Police Chief Benjamin Bassett said, "We are looking at this case from a number of angles: from an investigative standpoint, from a technology standpoint, and from an evidence-gathering standpoint." He said investigators are conducting ground searches, performing background checks, and doing interviews.

Anyone with information about what happened to Trello is urged to call the police. The tip line is 541-555-7788.

Meanwhile, a Firview man who identified himself as Trello's boyfriend is pushing for the case to be solved.

"I think the police could try harder to find her

killer," Daniel "Danny" Hitchens said. The eighteen-year-old said he had been dating Trello for a year. He told the *Times* he was the last one to see her alive at a party held at a friend's house, about six miles from where her body was found.

He said Trello became upset because someone she didn't like was also at the party. He said that they argued and she walked away. He thought she had gone to another room. "If I had known she was leaving, I could have stopped her."

Hitchens said they met in Spanish class at North Firview High School, and that he flirted with her for months before she agreed to date him. He said he "wasn't the greatest guy in the world" but said Trello loved him anyway.

Trello's best friend, Star Munroe, seventeen, said she was also supposed to be at the party, but came down with the flu.

"If I had been there, she wouldn't be dead," Munroe said. "When Layla left the party, I would have gone with her. Or I would have talked her out of leaving in the first place." She also described Hitchens as Trello's "on-again, off-again" boyfriend, saying their relationship was volatile. Asked if she thought Hitchens had anything to do with Trello's death, she declined to answer.

Police Chief Bassett said police have received a number of tips. "I hope people will be patient and let us do what we need to do," he said. "I sympathize with everyone feeling anxious, but all I can say is go about your daily routines. The general public has no reason to fear."

Chief Bassett refused to comment when asked about an incident last May involving Daniel Hitchens and his brother, Hunter, who is a year older. Both were charged with second-degree assault for an incident at a Jack in the Box. The case was ultimately dismissed when the victim did not show up in court.

"Don't believe everything you read," Daniel Hitchens told the *Times* when asked about the incident. "They said the kid almost died, which was a lie. He had minor injuries."

I raise my head from the viewer.

It doesn't take much reading between the lines to see who the prime suspect must have been. Danny Hitchens. Violent. Overly emotional. And by his own admission, "not the greatest guy."

I hit the button to make a printout.

CHAPTER ELEVEN

DON'T BELIEVE WHAT YOU READ

Saturday, August 29

I PRINT OUT ARTICLE after article, hoping all the pieces will make a bigger picture. I study grainy photographs of Layla and read the always flattering words used to describe her. Her next-door neighbor said she "had a constant smile." Vice Principal Barry—our current principal—told the *Times*, "She was a spirited young woman, a dedicated athlete, and, above all, a cherished part of our Bearcat family."

Most of the *Firview Times* coverage seems to consist of reprinting things Danny posted on his Facebook page.

Daniel "Danny" Hitchens updated his Facebook page Friday afternoon to tell people he planned to sell bracelets in Trello's honor for five dollars each.

Hitchens wrote, "All proceeds will go to the Trello family."

"Don't believe what you read in the newspapers or see on TV," Daniel "Danny" Hitchens wrote in a Facebook post. "Their sources aren't the police or people who knew Layla." He also said he wanted to clarify that he did not get into an argument with Trello before she disappeared. "We didn't really get into a fight. She was just peeved there were a couple of people at the party she didn't like."

With each passing week, there are fewer articles with less information.

Police Chief Bassett would not comment when asked if authorities had questioned any members of the Hitchens family. "We are working around the clock, literally, on a number of things," Chief Bassett said. "Prematurely releasing information about the case could harm the investigation."

Only as far as I can see, no additional information was ever released. Not a list of suspects. Not even the autopsy report.

Star Munroe told the *Times* that Hitchens had deleted his Facebook page because he was "being harassed." She also said Trello's family had asked her not to speak with the media anymore. "I'm listening to their wishes. So I'm not going to be saying anything more about the case."

Reached by phone, Daniel "Danny" Hitchens was also hesitant to go into detail. "I could jeopardize the investigation by saying too much, but I can say everyone loved Layla and no one hated her." He added, "I wish I could switch places with her. When she was murdered, so was I. I'm never gonna be normal again without her."

For longer and longer stretches, I find nothing. My eyes start to glaze over as I scan headlines for the words *Trello*, *murder*, or *teen*. The few articles are just a paragraph or two and basically say the case is still open.

Eventually I reach a year after Layla's murder, when the *Times* runs a story summarizing everything they've covered, but adds no new information. And then nothing. It seems like the story just reached a dead end.

I jump when Karen sets down some more microfiche.

"Sorry it took me a bit. I had to help a patron who wanted a book but could only remember it had a blue cover. I actually figured it out." After grinning triumphantly, Karen says, "I was also talking to my coworker. She said a couple of free local papers were publishing back then. *The Independent* and the *Valley Messenger*. I guess *The Independent* was kind of a one-man show covering local politics. Sounds like the *Messenger* mostly reviewed movies and places to eat. But she thought at least one of them might have covered the murder, since it was a big deal at the time. Both of them have since folded, but we have the microfiche." She leans over my shoulder. "Have you found anything interesting?"

"Yeah. It sounds like her boyfriend, this guy named Danny Hitchens, was the main suspect. But he was never arrested."

"Hitchens?" Karen purses her lips. "Like the auto dealerships? 'Hitch a ride with us'?"

That's why that name seemed vaguely familiar. Now I remember seeing commercials for Hitchens BMW, Hitchens Ford, and Hitchens Toyota while watching *Modern Family* reruns with Sequoia and Jasper. The commercials always end with the same older guy, Rich Hitchens, spouting his catchphrase.

Danny must be his son. And I'm guessing that, just like his name, Rich Hitchens is rich.

Karen gives the new microfiche a pat. "I'll let you get back to it."

With a sigh, I open them up. There's nothing about Layla in the *Valley Messenger*, just reviews of things to do on date night.

But *The Independent* lives up to its name. Whoever wrote the articles had strong opinions about the school board, the water bureau, the mayor, and the meter readers. The writer brought that same feeling of outrage to articles about Layla.

Who would know those woods well? The same woods that attract boys with .22-caliber rifles who like to plink at rabbits and squirrels? Which is the identical caliber of the bullet found in this innocent girl's chest.

That sparks an idea. Don't you hear about hunters accidentally shooting a person instead of an animal? When I google on my phone, I find stories of people being shot after being mistaken for a deer, a bear, or even a turkey. One woman was killed when a hunter thought her white glove was a deer's tail.

Layla was wearing white gloves that night, gloves that disappeared along with the rest of her clothes.

As time goes on, *The Independent*'s articles grow both vitriolic and focused on Danny, including one about the day of Layla's funeral that makes me do a double take. If it's true, it's explosive. I already know I will use it in a future podcast.

A few weeks after her funeral, there's this:

LAYLA TRELLO DESERVES JUSTICE

What dark secrets led to Layla Trello's deadly evening? The way this reporter sees it, Layla was not the random victim of a passing stranger, but the target of an elaborate, depraved plan carried out by someone who knew her and our area well.

First Layla was lured out of a wild teenage party. Before killing her, the killer probably did things that don't bear imagining. Afterward, he must have stuffed her broken body in his car trunk before transporting it to the desolate woods where he discarded it like a piece of trash.

Layla deserves justice, but instead the investigation into her shocking death has been bungled from the start by local cops who have virtually no experience in conducting a murder probe.

And *The Independent* has to ask: Were those cops willing to look the other way to protect someone whose family has money and connections?

CHAPTER TWELVE

DARK RED BLOOD
Saturday, August 29

ON MY WAY HOME from the library, I decide to visit Layla's grave. In the stillness of the cemetery, a spot of color again draws my eye to the place where she lies. After six days, it would be understandable if the flowers were withered and faded, or if the spray had disappeared completely.

Instead, the bouquet of pink roses has been totally ripped apart, reduced to brittle petals, crushed stems, and torn bits of tissue. Most of the mess is confined to Layla's grave, but it also spreads to the plots on either side. Could it have been an animal? As I get closer, I see the glint of broken glass. Someone has smashed the beer bottle.

Not knowing what else to do, I crouch down and start picking up the broken shards, holding them in a cupped palm. I carry them over to a garbage can a hundred feet away.

Back at Layla's grave, I'm lost in thought as I pluck up smashed stems, severed heads, bits of paper and plastic, and more glittering glass. What happened? This section has headstones that are flush with the ground so that the groundskeepers can just mow right over them. Was this destruction the result of a groundskeeper being lazy, an angry outburst from Layla's killer, or just some drunk jerk who had nothing better to do on a Friday night?

Somehow, a single pink rosebud on a three-inch stem has survived intact. I close my fist around the short stem, carry it home, and carefully lay it on my desk.

It's only then that I notice the cut on my palm, slowly pulsing dark red blood.

CHAPTER THIRTEEN

EVERYTHING YOU NEED
TO KNOW
Monday, August 31

EIGHT DAYS AGO, WHEN I stood six feet above where Layla's bones molder, I hadn't known she'd gone to North High.

Now, on my way to meet Jonas during free period, I think about how nearly twenty years ago, Layla must have traversed this same hall, her dark hair swinging. While I normally wear clothes that were made well before I was born, today I'm dressed the way Layla might have been: camo cargo pants, a plain black tee, a silver fish that dangles from a silver chain, and black low-top Chucks.

I walk by walls so scuffed that it's probably the same coat of paint as when Layla was here. Many of the teachers sitting at their desks or standing in their doorways are old enough that they could have taught her. Maybe even an atom or two floating around in this air was once in her lungs. I take a deep breath.

Suddenly the past feels so close.

But I'm invisible, a transfer student who knows no one. And Layla was, by all accounts, well-liked. Popular.

Chloe said this was my chance to start over, to be whoever I want to be. Why not emulate Kelley McBain? From listening to her for hours, I almost feel like I know her personally. I definitely know her personality. Brash, bold. She certainly wouldn't navigate this hall with hunched shoulders and eyes on the floor. I straighten up and let a half smile play on my lips. I relax my spine, let my hips and my hair move.

And just like that, I'm no longer invisible. Maybe I never was. After all, if I wasn't looking at anyone, how could I know if they were looking at me?

People I pass scan my face and clothes. I'm new, but obviously not a freshman. My clothes are unique. A few girls meet my gaze, their eyes narrowing a little. I can almost hear them trying to figure out who I am and where I fit into things. And a handful of guys look back, too, but their eyes get wider, as if they like what they see. A few even nod.

By the time I push the library door open, I feel like a different person. The door swishes shut behind me, leaving me in the relative quiet. In a way, it's a relief to drop Kelley's persona. Yet I also want to try it on again.

Jonas is sitting at the same table as before, in the very back. His head is bent over a book.

Inside my new red backpack, I have a book of my own. An oversize neon-green paperback caught my eye at the library. I recognized it as part of the popular Everything You Need to Know series of do-it-yourself guides. My mom had a couple at home. This one's titled *Everything You Need to Know...About Criminal Investigations*. It turned out to be the closest thing I could find to *How to Solve a Cold Case Murder When You're Only a High School Student*.

"Hey," Jonas says as I pull out the chair next to him.

"As instructed, I've done my homework." I set my laptop in front of him so he can see my logo. I decided to wait a few days to show it to him so I could be sure there was nothing he could find fault with.

Jonas leans forward on crossed arms, studying it carefully, which gives me a chance to study him. Today his sleeves are rolled up, revealing more faint white scars on his tanned forearms. He hits a few keys to shrink my image to the size of an actual thumbnail. The words are still clear.

Finally he sits back and nods. A piece of his gelled hair falls, accenting his left eye.

"It looks good. Even all uppercase, that font is super legible. The title makes it clear what it's about, and the tombstone underscores that. And of course by using her name you don't need to worry about anyone else having the same title."

"Thanks." I feel a surge of pride. "I've also started planning the first few episodes. I think I'll have the first word in every title be *the*, like The Couple, The Party, et cetera. The first one is going to be about what happened to Layla. The Crime. Some true-crime podcasters just read other people's reporting, but I want to do more. I mean, I can rewrite it, but I want to add something if I can. I could go back to the place where the party was, or where they found her body. Maybe interview the police. And I need to talk to the people who were her friends, especially the ones who were at the party. I'd also like to interview her family."

Jonas presses his lips together. Some sort of emotion flickers over his angular features.

"What?"

"What?" he says back.

"You obviously have some thoughts about my podcast."

"No." He shakes his head. "Never mind."

"You've already made it clear you don't like it being about a murder. That you think it's exploitative." If only someone else at school was a podcaster or Jonas was a different kind of person. He clearly doesn't understand.

He sighs. "Do you really think they're going to welcome this?"

"I'm sure the family wants to see justice done."

"I'm talking about more than her family and friends. You'll probably make whoever did it mad. Maybe they'll even try to stop you."

"That's never happened to Kelley McBain. She's the host of *Dead, Deader, Deadest.*" I pause then add, "At least I don't think it's happened. She's never talked about it."

"I still think you should choose a different topic." As Jonas speaks, he reaches into his backpack. He looks surprised when his hand comes out with a piece of paper folded into a square. He unfolds it. For a second, we both look at it.

It's a photocopy of a picture. A guy and girl, him in a suit and her in a shoulder-baring long dress. I think the guy is Jonas. The girl is Asian American. I think it's the girl who refused to talk to him, but I'm not certain. That's because someone has drawn *X*s over their eyes so ferociously that in one spot the paper is torn.

Written in all caps underneath is *YOU SHOULD BE DEAD!*

The word *YOU* has been underlined three times.

Jonas's face contorts as he crushes the note in his fist.

CHAPTER FOURTEEN

SHOW ME
Thursday, September 3

A FEW DAYS LATER, when I get home from school, I find the Amazon box with the microphone I ordered sitting on the front porch. Up in my room, I open the box. The mic only has three pieces, plus a USB cord, but it still takes time to figure out how to put it together. It stands on three metal legs and can be tilted at different angles. Once it's assembled, I plug it into my computer and open GarageBand. Under "input" I choose the name of the microphone.

That turns out to be the easiest part. As I move around the screen, yellow notes pop up explaining what each virtual button and dial does. Even the explanations are hard for me to follow.

At the top is a row of buttons. One's red, which at first I think means stop. But it's like the glowing red light in a real-life studio, indicating a recording in process. The stop button is actually a white square.

After taking a deep breath, I click the red button, ready to start reading my script. But my computer starts making an odd rhythmic click, like the ticking of a clock. I hit the white square to stop. Is something loose? I check the USB cord's connection at the mic and dongle, but both are secure. I start over, but so does the clicking.

Googling gets me nowhere. Finally, I break down and text Jonas, asking what I'm doing wrong. Instead of texting back, he video calls me.

I accept the call, already wondering if I should have kept trying to figure it out. "Hey, Jonas. Sorry to bug you."

"It's no problem. So you said your new mic is giving you feedback?" He's wearing a baseball cap backward. Is he in his room? I can just see the edge of what looks like a poster behind his right shoulder. I suddenly feel self-conscious about my room, with its bare walls.

"I'm trying to record my first podcast, and it keeps making this weird noise every time I start."

"Show me what's happening."

After switching to the phone's rear camera, I click the red button in GarageBand. The faint rhythmic sound starts up again. After a few seconds, I hit stop and flip the camera back around. "So is the mic defective? Maybe that's what I get for buying a cheap one." Since it's my dad's and Gretchen's money, I didn't want to spend too much.

Lifting one eyebrow, Jonas half smiles. He seems more relaxed than he does at school. "That's actually a metronome, like for musicians. It won't show up on the recording."

"Oh." I feel stupid, bugging him for nothing. "With a name like GarageBand, I guess I should have figured that out. Thanks. I'll let you go."

"Hey, wait!" he calls out before I can disconnect. "Let me at least walk you through how to turn it off, plus maybe a few other things. GarageBand isn't all that intuitive. I had to read a bunch of online tutorials, and the learning curve is steep. Remember, me helping you is why Ms. Kernow teamed us up."

Jonas walks me through several layers of menus to turn off the metronome. "Now try recording the first couple of lines. Then see how you like the sound and I can help you figure out how to adjust it."

"Okay." It feels way more personal to be talking while in each other's bedrooms, even if it's only virtually. I prop up the phone and put the script next to the mic. After taking a deep breath, I tap the red button. "Hello, armchair detectives. Welcome to the first episode of *Who Killed Layla Trello?* I'm your podcast host, Piper Gray." Then I hit stop.

When I look at my phone's screen, Jonas is watching me intently. "Okay," he says, "now play it back and see if you like the way it sounds."

When I do, it sounds tinny. I make a face. "Can you hear that? It sounds like there's a little bit of an echo."

He focuses his gaze past my shoulder. "How big is your space?"

"It's just my bedroom. Maybe ten by fifteen?" Flushing a little, I give the room a quick pan, thankful for Gretchen's rule about made beds.

"That might be too big. This is kind of a weird question, but how big is your closet? Could you record in there?"

"Hold on." I jump up and push all my clothes to one side of the rod. The other side has flat shelves. The bottom ones hold shoes and the top has folded sweaters. After gathering up my phone, laptop, microphone, and script, I carry them in. I shove a stack of sweaters aside so I can set up my laptop, then prop the phone against the screen, with the microphone next to it. When I close the door, I can already feel how much more hushed the space is.

"Welcome to the inner sanctum," I joke. Only it's not really a joke. Even though I know I'm alone in my closet, my clothes pressing against my back, it feels like Jonas is sharing the space with me. My face warms up. I hope he can't see it.

"What was that one sweater on top? It looked cool."

"This?" I hold it up. The boxy gray rag-wool cardigan is embroidered with red skiers, black trees, and red cross-stitching on the hem and collar. "Vintage Eddie Bauer. The zipper's metal, so it was probably made before 1965. And it was a steal at seven dollars."

"Do you get all your clothes at thrift stores?"

"Mostly. My mom didn't have much money, and she taught me that if you keep your eyes open you can find some cool stuff."

My mom is the one who taught me to look at every item hanging on a rack. Like if you don't check out the blue sweaters because you never wear blue, you might miss the amazingly embroidered sky-blue cardigan from the fifties, the one you could wear with the buttons running down the back. For once, thinking of my mom doesn't make me want to burst into tears.

"There's a thrift store downtown, but I don't think I've ever been in it." Jonas leans closer to the screen. "Why don't you record a new sample and see how it sounds?"

I do, and this time when I replay it, the faint echo is gone. I'm thinking it's good enough, but Jonas talks me through a bunch of steps that involve finding nested menus, wiggling sliders, and adjusting inputs. With each change, the sound improves.

He shows me how to see my voice on GarageBand. It's represented by a horizontal line with bursts of tight up-and-down scribbles, called waveforms. Words I emphasized have larger waveforms. Jonas walks me through how to cut out sections I don't want.

"What should I do if I make a mistake?"

"If it's small, or it's a small filler word or sound, like *ah* or *like*, just leave it in. If you take them all out, it sounds too scripted. If the mistake is bigger, just pause and repeat the sentence or paragraph correctly. Later, you can cut out the part you got wrong." He turns his head to the side, responding to something I can't see or hear. "Coming!" he calls, then turns back to me. "Sorry, I have to go down to dinner."

When I check the clock in the corner of the screen, I'm surprised to see how late it's gotten. "I probably should go help my stepmom with dinner." I press my palms together and give him a little bow. "Thank you so much for helping me. I'll bring it in tomorrow and you can tell me what you think."

All throughout dinner, I'm not only mentally going over everything I've learned, but I'm also thinking about Jonas. At school, he always looks closed off, never meeting anyone's eyes, but this afternoon a whole range of expressions crossed his face.

After dinner I go back upstairs and start over. I end up recording it four times. Each time, I'm a little more relaxed and need my script a little less. I learn to hit save a lot. The last recording is the one I edit, cutting around the edges for a cleaner—but not too clean—product.

It's after midnight, but finally it's done. The first episode of *Who Killed Layla Trello?*

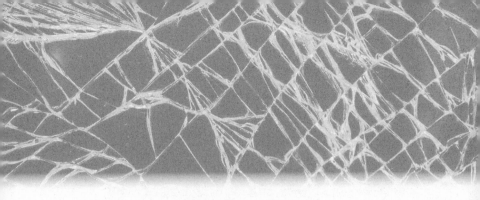

CHAPTER FIFTEEN

TRANSCRIPT OF EPISODE 1
OF *WHO KILLED LAYLA TRELLO?*:
"THE CRIME"
Air date: September 13

HELLO, ARMCHAIR DETECTIVES! WELCOME to the first episode of *Who Killed Layla Trello?* I'm your podcast host, Piper Gray. Almost two decades ago, seventeen-year-old Layla Trello disappeared from a Halloween party here in Firview, Oregon. Nearly two weeks later her body was found in the forest a few miles away. She had been shot to death. And no one has ever been arrested for her murder.

So who killed Layla Trello? Was it a scorned boyfriend? A random stranger? An out-of-season hunter? Or could her murder be tied to something bigger? Listen in as I try to figure out what happened. I'm doing research, asking questions, and trying to track down those who might know the answers.

So while Layla Trello's case may have gone cold, it doesn't have to stay cold. As we examine what happened, maybe we can breathe new life into her case.

Now before we go any further, let me remind you that since we're talking about murder, you're going to hear some details about violence. Listener discretion is advised.

Like I said, my name's Piper Gray. I just started my senior year at North Firview High in Southern Oregon. Firview is located about forty minutes north of the California border.

A few weeks ago, I was walking through Firview's Skyline Cemetery when I came across Layla's grave. I noticed it because someone had left flowers and a beer on her grave marker. Layla Trello was only seventeen years old when she died. And when I googled "Layla Trello," I learned about her murder. Almost twenty years later, her case is still unsolved.

Immediately, I had questions. What had Layla been like? Why was she killed?

The first question was easier to answer. The second is still a mystery.

Layla lived with her parents and her younger sister, Aubrey, in an upscale neighborhood. Her dad, John, was a banker. Her mom, Cindy, was a homemaker who also did volunteer work.

Layla was about five foot five, with dark shoulder-length hair she pulled back in a ponytail when she ran. Which was a lot. She ran both track and cross-country, and while she wasn't a star, she was still quite good. Good enough that there was talk of scouts checking her out for small college teams. Her grades were mostly Bs, again good, but maybe not good enough for a top-level university.

Layla was something of a chameleon, fitting in wherever she was. She was an athlete, but she also liked to party. She did well in school, but she was also popular. Reading between the lines, I'm guessing she wanted what every teenager wants: to be unique while also being accepted.

Layla had a boyfriend, another senior named Danny Hitchens. When Layla disappeared, he told the media they had been dating seriously for about a year. But her best friend, Star Munroe, said they had more of an on-again, off-again relationship. From what I've read, Danny had a reputation as a slacker in school. Outside of school, he, together with his older brother, Hunter, sometimes got in trouble for brawling.

That year, Halloween fell on a Friday. And that night, Layla went with Danny to a Halloween party. The kind of party that can only happen because the parents are out of town. Several dozen kids were there, and there were hookups and breakups, drinking and maybe some drugs, and even a fight or two.

One of those fights was between Layla and Danny. He's never said publicly what the argument was about, and sometimes he's even denied they argued at all. What we do know is that she left the party after they spoke.

What happened after that is a mystery, with no suspects, no motive, and no way of knowing how she got to where her body was found.

Did someone follow her out, perhaps to attempt again something she rejected?

Was she picked up by a stranger who pretended to offer help?

Or was she forcibly kidnapped?

There are numerous theories.

But no one knows the truth. Or rather, someone knows. Maybe many someones. But they haven't come forward.

What had Layla and Danny fought about? Some people said it was over Layla catching Danny's older brother, Hunter, kissing a girl. A girl who wasn't his girlfriend. Hunter's real girlfriend was Star Munroe, Layla's best friend, who was home sick that night.

Danny said that after he realized Layla was gone, he drove around but didn't find her. He claimed he decided she must have walked home. He himself went home and didn't tell anyone what was going on.

Cindy and John believed Layla had spent the night at Star's house. It was only after they called Star around lunchtime the next day that they realized their daughter was missing. Her disappearance wasn't reported to authorities until midafternoon. By then the trail was already growing cold. The police searched. The family searched. As the hours and then the days went by, the police brought in a dog handler. The family consulted a psychic.

Twelve agonizing days went by. Twelve days filled with wild rumors. Some people said Layla had run off with an older man. Others thought she killed herself. Some believed she had been kidnapped by a biker gang. There were tales that she had been buried in a sewer pipe or ground up in a wood chipper by a meth dealer. One theory had Layla dying from a drug overdose, with the other partygoers panicking and disposing of her body.

Then someone collecting bear grass in the forest found Layla's body next to a stream called Gilkey Creek. At the time police speculated that the body had been dumped into the stream and then washed up on the bank. The Halloween party had had a seventies theme, so Layla had left wearing flared pants and a denim vest with fringe. Those clothes were never found. Neither was her purse, her puffer coat, or her white gloves.

The cause of death was a single .22-caliber bullet to the chest. It severed an artery near Layla's heart. Police believed she had been killed the night she disappeared, but they didn't say much more. The full autopsy report, including whether there were any drugs or alcohol in Layla's system, or whether she was sexually assaulted, has never been released.

A lot of people blamed her boyfriend, Danny. And it's a sad truth that if a woman or girl ends up dead, at least fifty percent of the time, it's a partner or an ex-partner who did it. Not a stranger. Let me pause here to say that if you are experiencing domestic violence and need someone to talk to, please call the National Domestic Violence Hotline at 1-800-799-7233.

If a killer is a stranger, they are almost always men, and most of the time, it's women they go looking for. Women they go hunting. Women who are most vulnerable. Take Layla, walking home in the dark, at a time when everyone else was in bed. She was emotional, maybe a little drunk, definitely tired, and completely alone. Take Layla, which is what someone did.

You have reached the end of the first episode of *Who Killed Layla Trello?* Be sure to like, review, and subscribe wherever you usually get your true-crime podcasts. And if you have a tip you'd like to share, find the Who Killed Layla Trello? Facebook page or email me at WhoKilledLaylaTrello@gmail.com. I'll be uploading new episodes weekly. My next episode will be all about Layla. Who she was and who she might have been.

CHAPTER SIXTEEN

FULL OF EMOTION
Friday, September 4

JONAS SITS ACROSS FROM me in the library, listening to the first episode of *Who Killed Layla Trello?* with his eyes closed. The episode is just ten minutes long, but somehow it seems like he's already been listening for an hour. I watch his eyes move under his lids, his brows rise and then pull together, his lips purse or twist into a frown. He's lost in his own world. A world I created.

Finally, Jonas opens his eyes and pulls out his earbuds. "You really applied everything we talked about." After a pause, he adds, "Technically, it's very good."

I know a diss when I hear one. So much for feeling like a team last night. "And other than technically?"

He draws a deep breath. "Violence isn't entertainment."

I cross my arms. "Wait a minute. What's your podcast about again?"

"Sports."

"Which sports?" I demand, even though I know the answer. "Swimming? Fencing? Tennis? Gymnastics?"

"Team sports. It's a look back at some of the best games ever played."

"And is one of them football?" I don't wait for him to answer my rhetorical question. "Are you trying to tell me *sports* aren't violent? Some fans even celebrate hard hits. No one's celebrating Layla's death."

"People don't get killed playing football."

"Aren't a lot of ex–football players getting diagnosed with brain damage?" I remember something my dad said over the weekend. "And aren't players getting bigger and the hits harder?"

"Football can be like the most complicated chess game." Jonas holds up both hands, miming surrender. "But you're right. It can also have this whole caveman, gladiator vibe. Still at its core, it's about strategy and teamwork. Plus I cover more sports than just football."

"And are they any better? Even I know that some hockey fans just go to see the fights. Basketball's a contact sport. What about that guy who just broke his leg? And a baseball player could get hit in the face with a hundred-mile-an-hour fastball. Violence, violence, violence."

In a weird way, I'm actually starting to enjoy myself.

Then Jonas says, "That's the world's best athletes choosing to pit themselves against one another. Not some poor girl getting kidnapped and murdered."

"Layla deserves justice. And if I can get people talking about what happened, that might happen."

He just presses his lips together.

"Look," I say. "We're both making podcasts that don't appeal to the other person. Can't you just look past the content and help me with how it's presented?"

After a moment, Jonas nods. He spends the next thirty minutes helping me fine-tune it.

"It seems like most podcasts begin and end with music," I say. "Kelley McBain probably paid someone to write her theme song, but I can't afford that."

"It might be just off the shelf." He opens a menu I haven't seen before. "GarageBand has dozens of prerecorded music snippets you can use." After plugging in his wired earbuds, he offers me one. As we listen to various loops, I'm aware of his chest rising and falling, of the moments when he closes his eyes.

The loops can be sorted according to the feelings they evoke, such as relaxed, cheerful, intense, or dark. Orchestral Strings Six sounds moody and a little bit scary. It's perfect.

We play around with fading the music in and out, and when it should be under my words. Free period flies by. When it ends, we are more the people we were last night.

Walking home from school, I start listening to an episode

of Jonas's podcast chosen at random. The game he walks listeners through is a surprise. It isn't about two famous professional teams, big men who get paid a lot of money. Instead it's about a basketball game that happened four years ago in Nebraska. A *high school* girls' basketball game.

And his guest was the star of that game. Now she's a college student, with no plans to play professionally.

A week ago, I wouldn't have been interested at all. Today what catches my attention is not so much the content, but the technical aspects. How does Jonas pace himself? How does he use music? How does his voice sound? Do his *T*s and *P*s pop too much? Is there any echo? Does his sound level match that of his guest? How much of their conversation is unscripted banter?

But slowly, I find myself falling under his spell. Jonas sounds engaged. Happy. And his interest begins to make me interested.

For him, sports are exciting. Full of emotion. An escape from whatever troubles people are having in their own lives. And even though he only observed the game they're discussing, Jonas obviously feels a connection.

Excitement, emotion, escape, connection. The same emotions I'm trying to make people feel when they listen to my podcast.

Are our two podcasts really so different?

Are we?

CHAPTER SEVENTEEN

WISH I COULD TALK TO YOU
Monday, September 7

ALTHOUGH MY UNPUBLISHED FIRST podcast referenced a Gmail address and a Facebook page, they don't actually exist. Yet. I set them up over the long weekend.

The Gmail address is fairly easy. The Facebook page takes longer. I use the same school photo of Layla that appeared in every news article. Is it under copyright? I have no clue how to figure that out and decide it probably doesn't matter.

For the page's description, I write, "Dedicated to solving the murder of Layla Trello. Feel free to share memories of Layla or post links to information about the case. If you knew Layla or have a tip, DM me."

Layla must have lived in my general neighborhood, but where? I type *John Trello* into an online people finder.

It's weird to see that the Trello house is actually only four blocks from here.

Even though it's Labor Day, I have the house to myself. Dad and Gretchen took Jasper and Sequoia to the county fair. I said no when they asked if I wanted to go. It was clearly a big family tradition—Jasper had been talking nonstop all week about petting lambs and eating elephant ears—and it just felt like I probably wouldn't fit in. I'm too old to be a kid and too young to be an adult.

So there's no one to ask why I'm wearing sunglasses and a baseball cap pulled low as I walk out the door. In a few blocks, I see the Trello house on the corner. It's Craftsman-style, two stories tall, dark teal with white trim. A half dozen concrete stairs lead up to a big front porch. As I get closer, it's clear everything has fallen into disrepair. The yard is half weeds. Emerald green moss grows on the risers of the concrete steps. On one side of the house, the paint is peeling.

The driveway is empty. If there was a car, would I risk going up the stairs, knocking on the big oak door, and waiting for Cindy or John Trello to answer? The whole prospect seems terrifying. Today, at least, I don't have to decide. I turn around and start for home.

This weekend, I've read more of the *Everything You Need to Know* book and worked on my notes for the second episode. I've also been thinking about what I should do next. I definitely want to talk to Layla's family, but that's too daunting for my first interview.

Danny Hitchens? Even if he didn't kill Layla, he's probably not going to welcome renewed attention to the case. I remember all those articles hinting that he liked to solve problems with his fists.

I want to interview the people who were at the party, but it's hard to know who was there. I've only seen a few first names, probably because most of them were minors.

The best place to start seems like Layla's best friend, Star Munroe. Back at home, I google her but don't find anything more recent than a dozen years ago.

On Facebook, I find a couple of Star Munroes, but after scrolling through their photos and reading bios set firmly in other states, it seems likely they just happen to have the same name.

Maybe she's friends with one of the Trellos, either the parents or Layla's sister, Aubrey? I type in *Trello* in Facebook's search bar. It's not that common a name. Cindy Trello is one of the results. I'm sure it's the right Cindy Trello because her Facebook profile shows her with her arm around Layla.

But she's not the only Trello family member with a Facebook profile.

I suck in my breath. Because Layla's on there, too.

And when I click her profile, it's not one of those *In Memory* pages. It's her real page, but of course with no personal updates after her death. It was created back in the day when Facebook was new and privacy was looser. Back when Layla was alive, and since then no one has told

Facebook she's dead. Each of her old posts has dozens of comments, most made soon after she died. Some clearly from strangers, talking about how Layla's an angel now, or how they are praying for her soul and/or for justice.

Others seem to be from friends, explaining how bereft they are or mentioning shared memories. "I still miss you every second." "I think of you every day." "I still remember that time by the river."

One's from her mother. "Happy birthday, honey. I miss you so much. I'm going to make your favorite German chocolate cake today."

I keep scrolling down the page, skimming over comments. Is each one a clue or just a stranger who felt a connection to a dead girl?

A month after Layla died, there's a comment from a Hitchens. But it's not Danny. It's from his brother, Hunter. "If I tried to make a list of all the ways you changed my life, it would be so long I'd still be writing it years later. You're in heaven now, so I'm sure you understand everything. I know you will always be watching over us, your family and friends. You have left a lasting impact on all our lives. You will never be forgotten."

Danny actually did leave a comment, right after Layla's body was found. It's so short my eyes skipped past it the first time through. "I wish I could hug you and talk to you." I try clicking on his name, but it seems his Facebook account, the one that Star told the newspaper he had deleted, remains so.

As I scroll back to the top of the page, my eyes light on another note. It's only two years old.

"Thinking of you today. I wish I could talk to you someplace besides in my head." It's from a Star, but Star Stoddard, not Star Munroe. I click through to her page. Unlike Layla's, it's not open to everyone. I can see some biographical information, her profile picture, a list of her friends, and that's it. I squint at the picture, trying to imagine the woman shown on horseback as the teenager I've seen in a few group photos with Layla. I think it's her. And how many people named Star could live in Firview?

Her profile shows she works at a big department store. Despite the different last name, it says "single" under relationship status. In addition to Layla, she has eighty-six friends. I click the button to send her a direct message.

"Hello, my name is Piper Gray. I'm a student at North High. I'm reaching out to you because I understand you were Layla Trello's best friend. I don't know if this happened when you were a student, but as a senior, I have to work on a year-long passion project. I want to do a podcast about Layla, in the hope of bringing new attention to her case. While I realize it might be painful for you, I would love to talk to you about what she was like, and what you think might have happened. It doesn't seem fair that her killer is free and her case seems to have been forgotten. Maybe together we can change that."

After dinner that night, I go in my closet and record episode 2.

CHAPTER EIGHTEEN

PARTIAL TRANSCRIPT OF EPISODE 2 OF *WHO KILLED LAYLA TRELLO?*: "THE VICTIM"
Air date: September 13

...BEFORE I LOOK AT what Layla was like as a person, let me address some objections you may have. Layla was young, white, middle-class, pretty, and popular. Basically, she was the perfect victim, media-wise. Her disappearance and death attracted the kind of attention you probably wouldn't get if you were poor, disabled, older, homeless, or not white. And of course that's not fair.

But I didn't pick Layla to be the focus of this podcast because she was pretty, young, and white. I chose her because she was from the town where I now live and was my age when she died. In fact, she lived in my neighborhood and went to my school. So I relate to her in personal ways.

And even if Layla's case got a lot of attention seventeen years ago, she's now mostly forgotten. I've searched for recent media coverage, but there isn't much. Sometimes on the anniversary of her death, our local paper, the *Firview Times*, has briefly mentioned that her case remains unsolved.

In trying to figure out what happened, I've been reading about how the police solve murders. Their first step is to focus on the victim. You might think it's not fair to put Layla under the microscope. It feels like saying it's her fault. But in order to understand why the killer decided she had to die, investigators need to understand her.

Did someone perceive Layla as an obstacle? A threat? Did she have something they wanted?

Was Layla specifically selected by the killer, or was her death simply the result of opportunity and circumstance? In other words, was this a wrong-time, wrong-place killing, with Layla just unlucky enough to cross paths with a killer?

The neighborhood she disappeared from is considered safe, with big houses and wide streets. But a drunk girl walking alone at night might have looked like prey to someone who thought of himself as a hunter.

And speaking of hunters, many use a .22-caliber to hunt deer, squirrel, and other small game. Layla's body was found in the forest with a .22 slug in her heart. What if that was no coincidence? If she somehow had ended up in the woods after leaving the party, could she have been mistaken for an animal?

If authorities had found her clothes, gunshot residue on

them could have offered clues about how far away the killer was when Layla was shot. But her clothes and purse were never found.

If Layla's death was deliberate, I've read that the decision to kill is usually made just prior to the murder. To find the killer, we should look at who the victim came into contact with in the last few days, hours, and even minutes before the murder.

But in the last seventy-two hours of Layla's life, she literally crossed paths with hundreds of people—her fellow classmates.

Experts also say most murders are the result of interpersonal conflict. A murder might be the killer's attempt to solve a problem with the victim. So it's unlikely the killer was someone Layla just passed in the hall. Instead, it was probably someone she spent time with. Was the killer at the party that night?

The police also had to have considered whether Layla's lifestyle put her in contact with people who could pose a physical threat. At first you might think that as a high school student and competitive runner who lived in a good neighborhood, Layla had a low-risk lifestyle. But by all accounts, drugs were being used around her. Maybe even by her. It was not much of a secret that her boyfriend, Danny Hitchens, occasionally used drugs. It was even insinuated that he sold them.

As I said in episode 1, to this day the authorities have never released the full results of Layla's autopsy. Is it because she was impaired? The beer I found on her grave supports the articles citing anonymous sources who said she was drinking at the party.

So if her drinking wasn't a secret, why not release the results? Was there something more in her system, and were they trying not to embarrass her family?

Does it matter if Layla was drunk *and* high? It doesn't make the killer any less guilty. You can't blame the victim. Although it's true she would have been less watchful, less alert. Not thinking as well. How security conscious was she that night? Did she walk with her keys between her fingers, ready to confront anyone who tried to hurt her?

If you dig a little deeper when you're looking for photos of her, if you look for, say, L period Trello or Trello comma Layla, you can find photos of her running. She runs with numbers pinned to her chest and back, her arms bent at ninety-degree angles, her hands in loose fists. In one, she's crossing the finish line, her right hand punching the air in triumph.

Like I said in the first episode, Layla was fast. Did she try to run from her killer?

I imagine Layla after she stormed out of the house that night. Once she shuts the door behind her, the noise of the party immediately drops. It rained that morning but had stopped by afternoon. That night it's unseasonably warm. As she moves down the sidewalk, the long fringe on her vest moves in time with her steps. The smell of wet dirt and pavement mixes with the fug of rotting leaves.

It's two AM, and Layla is completely alone. Until suddenly she isn't.

Until someone makes her disappear.

CHAPTER NINETEEN

BAD NEWS
Wednesday, September 16

IT'S BEEN THREE DAYS since I uploaded the first two episodes of *Who Killed Layla Trello?* Three days and it's gotten thirty-six downloads. My feelings about that number go back and forth. Thirty-six is nothing when you compare it to the hundreds of thousands who listen to *Dead, Deader, Deadest*. And one of the thirty-six is me. But that still means thirty-five people, maybe people I don't even know, have listened to it. Even Kelley McBain had to start someplace.

In Creative Writing, I check the Who Killed Layla Trello? Facebook page on my phone, which is hidden in my lap. I figure I'm safe since Mrs. Wharton is talking about her plans for the weekend, even though it's only Wednesday. She's going to Portland for a concert and then some barhopping. Some days she seems more peer than mentor. Like one of us, only with more money, her own car, and a license that isn't lying when it says she's over twenty-one.

No one has commented or sent me a DM. Yet.

But when I click over to my personal page, there's a direct message from Star Stoddard. My finger trembles as I open it. What if she feels the way Jonas does?

When I open it, she's agreed to talk to me next Thursday. She doesn't say much more, but it's huge.

Jonas's foot bumps mine. "Piper?" I realize this is not the first time Mrs. Wharton has said my name. "Piper?" A few people are giggling, a few look sympathetic, and a few are quickly hiding their own phones, just glad it wasn't them.

"Sorry." I tuck my phone in my pocket while simultaneously trying to look attentive. And usually I am. Creative Writing is my favorite class. Almost everything I write comes back with an A on the top and red stars marking parts Mrs. Wharton especially likes. Sometimes the whole page is as starred as the night sky.

"I was asking if you wanted to share what you wrote for the six-word memoir assignment."

Ernest Hemingway supposedly wrote a six-word story: "For Sale: baby shoes, never worn."

Our story was supposed to be about ourself. I suddenly wish mine wasn't so honest. Feeling my face warm, I read, "Forget or remember? I can't decide." Mrs. Wharton had promised she wouldn't ask what our stories meant, which is why I risked writing that.

"Ooh, nice!"

I feel a little glow of pride.

Most of the others who volunteer after me seem to have written stuff like "Life is often a pretentious game." Jonas is not one of the volunteers. When I see him in the hall, he walks with his head down. I've never seen him walking with anyone.

That afternoon, a girl approaches me. It's Alice, the one who made a point of not speaking to Jonas in the library.

"Oh my God, I've been listening to your podcast. That is you, right? I mean your name is Piper Gray, right, and the girl on the podcast said she goes to North, and of course you're the only one here with that name, but I still can't quite believe I'm talking to you." Alice speaks in what seems like a single breath, only stopping when she runs out of air.

"Um, thank you?" I say. Is this how Kelley McBain feels when she meets a fan? And does that mean I have fans now? I suppress a grin.

"My name's Alice." Her eyes widen. "How did you get all that information?"

Google and the library doesn't sound all that exciting. I find myself arching an eyebrow. "I have my ways."

She shivers in delight. "I can't wait to tell everyone that it *is* you."

At lunch, Alice always sits at a crowded table in the middle of the cafeteria. Just during the time we've been talking, a half dozen people have waved at her or called her name. If she talks the podcast up, it could really grow listenership.

"Thank you." Channeling my inner Kelley McBain, I bestow a smile on her. This morning I winged out my eyeliner, the way Kelley does.

Alice is still regarding me as if I'm something special. "I love your shirt. Is it vintage?"

I nod. That's one way of describing it. The white cotton peasant blouse with red embroidery and a smocked neckline and sleeves came from Goodwill. Maybe my vintage clothes will be my trademark, just like Kelley's winged eyeliner and V-neck tops are hers.

"One other thing," Alice says.

The smile drops from her face and I brace myself. "Uh-huh?"

"I know you're new here." She leans closer. "But take my advice and stay away from Jonas. He's bad news."

CHAPTER TWENTY

ALL METAL AND PLASTIC
Thursday, September 17

WHEN I WALK INTO the library, Jonas is already sitting in our usual spot. Sometimes he helps me with my podcast, or he shares what he's working on. Other days we work on our own homework.

"I saw you talking to Alice yesterday," he says as I sit down.

Yesterday the warning bell had rung, and Alice turned away before I could explain that Jonas was just assigned to help me with my podcast.

"She really likes the show. And she's talking it up." The number of downloads doubled overnight.

"Well, she doesn't talk to me anymore, as you probably noticed." Jonas sighs. "In fact, she hates me."

I remember how Alice refused to acknowledge him.

The defaced photo is in his backpack. Her warning to me. I take a breath. "Because you broke up with her?"

"I only wish that was the reason." His mouth twists. "But no. Alice hates me because I was the one behind the wheel when an accident killed her best friend."

It feels like the world just tilted. "Wait, what?"

Jonas looks down at his lap, his palm rubbing his knee. "About a year ago, I started dating this girl. Suzie Yang. She was Alice's best friend. At first it was," he pauses, "exciting. It got intense, really fast. Then pretty soon if Suzie texted me and I didn't text her back right away, she'd accuse me of not loving her enough. Sometimes even of seeing someone else. Which I wasn't. We were always breaking up and making up. The night of the accident, Suzie kept insisting I pull over and let her out. She had already unbuckled her seat belt. But we were out in the country. It wouldn't have been safe. I told her I was just going to take her home. Then she grabbed the wheel. That's when I lost control of the car and hit a tree. They had to use the jaws of life to get us out. But it was too late for Suzie." He closes his eyes, but they still move underneath his lids. "And too late for my leg."

"Your leg?" I echo faintly. The news is coming so fast I can't hold on to any one revelation. Jonas's girlfriend died? In the car he was driving? He's missing a leg?

He leans down and raps his calf. It makes a hollow sound. "I'm all metal and plastic from my knee down. They told me I was lucky because I was able to keep the knee.

Lucky. When my girlfriend was dead and half my leg was gone. Some days it felt like I died when she did. I lost my girlfriend, I lost friends, I lost getting to play sports, I lost the chance of college scholarships for playing. I don't drive anymore."

I grab on to this last bit because it seems the easiest. "You're not allowed to?"

"No. It was ruled an accident." He rubs his knee. "I just start to shake every time I get behind the wheel."

This explains Jonas's awkward gait, the trouble he had getting to his feet in the cemetery, the scars on his face and arms. Maybe even why I never see him in the cafeteria.

"Why don't you just tell Alice that the accident was Suzie's fault?"

"Why cause anyone any more pain? And I don't think it would make her feel any better. Alice could either be super depressed that her best friend is dead or blame me for it and be super angry. Being angry is easier. When you're angry, it can almost feel powerful. I just wish I had someone I could be angry at, besides myself." His exhale is so heavy it shakes. "I never talk about this stuff, but I knew you would understand. You know what it's like to lose someone you love."

It takes me a second to realize what he's referring to.

"My mom," I finally say.

Nothing is as uncomplicated as Jonas thinks it is.

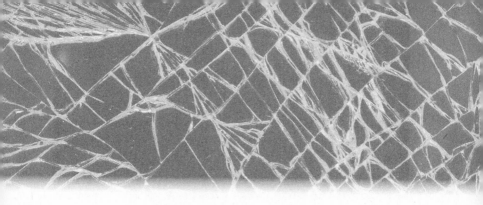

CHAPTER TWENTY-ONE

PARTIAL TRANSCRIPT OF EPISODE 3 OF *WHO KILLED LAYLA TRELLO?*: "THE INVESTIGATION"
Air date: September 20

...NO MATTER HOW OLD a murder case is, if it's unsolved, the police still consider it open. When I e-mailed the Firview Police Department about Layla's case, all I got was an e-mailed reply from their public affairs officer, saying, "Given that there is an ongoing investigation into the homicide of Layla Trello, only limited information can be provided." The statement then listed facts like when and where Layla's body was found. But nothing more.

At the time of Layla's death it was reported that the Firview Police Department had about thirty-five officers. What they didn't have was a full-time homicide squad, so on the rare occasion that a body did turn up—back then, the city averaged about three homicides a year—every one of the half dozen detectives was called in.

The police scoured the neighborhood where the party was held, and then later the forest where Layla's body was found. But the only clue they ever found, or at least the only one ever reported in the media, was Layla's phone. It was discovered in a puddle not far from the house where the party occurred. The police checked to see what cell towers it had pinged, but once the party was underway, the phone had stayed in the same location.

When they discovered it, the phone's screen was smashed. Does that mean Layla had fought with someone? Or did being under the influence make her clumsy? It would have slowed her thinking, might have made her careless or impulsive.

Detectives attended both Layla's funeral and burial, believing the killer might as well. They were in street clothes, but they still looked like cops. They even took pictures of the people who came to the service and, later, the cemetery.

For a week or two, detectives also sat outside North High in their unmarked cars, watching students troop in and out. They talked to school officials about students with an inclination for trouble. They asked other teens if they knew anyone who might be jealous of or angry with Layla.

It didn't take long for rumors to start flying. Many students wondered if the killer was another student, someone who walked the same halls as them.

Everyone denied knowing what happened. Her family.

Her friends. The other students. The people at the party. And Layla's on-again, off-again boyfriend, Danny Hitchens.

Out of the thousands of words I have read in my research, only one local publication, *The Independent*, directly suggested a possible link between Layla's death and Danny Hitchens. And its reporting was explosive. It also ceased publication just a few weeks after publishing the following article.

EXCLUSIVE: SUSPECTED DRUG OVERDOSE AT HOME OF MURDERED TEEN'S BOYFRIEND

The Independent is living up to its name, the only publication brave enough to publish the explosive allegations about the young man many savvy observers consider the prime suspect in the grisly murder of slaughtered teen beauty Layla Trello.

Shortly after Layla's body was found discarded in the woods, and on the day the seventeen-year-old was laid to rest, police and paramedics responded to a 911 call reporting a possible drug overdose. The call came from the family home of the young man who has claimed to be Layla's boyfriend.

A police scanner report at 10:46 AM said an ambulance was requested at a North Firview residence. Records show the property is owned by Richard "Rich" Hitchens. The senior Hitchens lives up to his nickname, owning five wildly successful auto dealerships in the local area. His older son, Hunter, nineteen years old, shares the family home.

His younger son, Danny Hitchens, eighteen, was

Layla's boyfriend, although her friends have described the relationship as rocky. In addition, Danny has claimed he may have been the last person to see her alive, not seeming to realize how damning that claim is.

The report said the ambulance was for someone who had suffered a possible drug overdose. A representative of Mercy Medical Center said someone with the last name Hitchens was in the emergency room Saturday morning but stonewalled when pressed for further information. Hospital higher-ups later claimed no one with the name Hitchens was admitted as an inpatient on Saturday.

In response to a message left by this reporter on his Facebook page, Danny Hitchens said, "Nothing happened at the house yesterday. It was a false alarm. Just more rumors."

Earlier in the year, police arrested the two brothers on felony assault charges after an altercation at a fast-food restaurant left a third young man injured, or, as a witness described it, "beaten to a bloody pulp." The same witness described the ringleader of the assault as "the younger one." The charges were ultimately dismissed when the victim did not show up in court. Jaded readers will be forgiven for thinking money may have changed hands.

This curious incident at the Hitchens residence occurred around the time of Layla's funeral. A source says the Trellos made it clear to the Hitchens family that Danny was not welcome at the funeral.

CHAPTER TWENTY-TWO

GREED, DESIRE, OR POWER

Monday, September 21

TODAY I'M WEARING AN outfit that's a deliberate study in echoes and contrasts. My black knit peplum top has white polka dots the size of quarters. My pants are black-and-white-checkered, the checks the size of a checkerboard's.

"Vroom, vroom," Jonas says, waving a hand to indicate my pants, which I now realize do look like a racing flag. But he sounds appreciative, not mocking. He's a little more relaxed around me now that I know his secret.

You don't get to be like Kelley McBain by doing what everyone else does. And it's not only my thrift store finds that are getting me noticed. It's the podcast. Every day, the number of listeners grows. More kids have stopped me in the hall to comment on it.

"I listened to your latest episode this morning," Jonas says.

After working on it all weekend, I uploaded it last night. The first episode has now been downloaded over five hundred times. "I thought you didn't like true-crime podcasts."

"I still don't. But this one's different."

"Because it's about someone who went to school here?"

"Because I'm supposed to be helping you make it better, at least on a technical level."

I feel deflated. "Was something off? The music? It was harder to fade in and out without you helping me."

Jonas sighs. "Actually, it sounded pretty good. My thought was about the actual story. The, um, case. I think there's an angle you're overlooking. But"—he shakes a warning finger at me—"you can't air it without any proof."

"Okay." I hide my prideful smile. It's a real coup, getting Jonas interested. "What's the angle?"

"You talked a lot about the other students who would have crossed paths with Layla here at school. But about five percent of the people in this building aren't students. They're adults."

I consider this, my eyes narrowing. "Nobody's talked about any adults being at the party."

"But Layla was killed after she *left* the party," Jonas points out. "Her death could be completely unconnected."

Jonas has an interesting point. What if her death had

nothing to do with her being at the party or leaving it? "I've been reading about murder investigations. I guess there are three basic reasons people commit murder: greed, desire, or power. But pretty much any adult would be more powerful than Layla was. And it wasn't like she had a car, or expensive jewelry, or a ton of cash. So that pretty much leaves some kind of a relationship."

Jonas purses his lips. "And if Layla had a relationship with an adult, even if it was consensual, it would still mean that adult could go to jail."

His idea reminds me of something I read. I do a quick search of my notes.

"Principal Barry—he was vice principal back then—was quoted as saying Layla 'was a spirited young woman, a dedicated athlete, and, above all, a cherished part of our Bearcat family.'" I lift my head. "Does *spirited* sound like code for someone who gets sent to the office a lot?"

Jonas raises one eyebrow. "If things back then are the same as they are now, it would have been the vice principal who handled discipline."

"In other words, Principal Barry."

"But that's only one guy," he points out. "And dozens of adults must have worked here then, just like now. Probably forty percent are men."

I'm still mulling that over when I check my e-mails at lunch. My excitement builds when I see two in the podcast account. One is from a man who says he is a former North student. "I was at the party, but I didn't even see Layla, so I'm afraid I can't help you. A lot of people were drunk off their faces. Including me, I'm sorry to say."

The subject for the second reads "Important." I click on it and read: "You need to stop this podcast about Layla Trello. You don't want to end up like her."

And the return address is youareindanger at an e-mail service I don't recognize.

I read the address again, only with spaces. *You are in danger.*

CHAPTER TWENTY-THREE

WE KNEW EVERYTHING

Thursday, September 24

I'M WALKING TO STAR'S apartment after school, when I notice a guy with a shaved head and aviator sunglasses walking on the other side of the street. While he's not looking at me, he's been keeping my pace for at least a couple of blocks. He's solid, his plain black T-shirt revealing muscled arms. I feel like I've seen him someplace before, again in the background.

Then he takes out his phone and starts tapping it. I tell myself I am imagining it. I'm just spooked by what was probably a prank e-mail. I answered it with a single question: "Who are you?" But my reply just bounced back. I didn't say anything about it to Jonas.

The man stays put while I climb the outdoor stairs to the third floor of the apartment building.

"Come on in." Star steps back from the door of 3C. She's bone-thin, with shoulder-length hair that was dyed blond months ago.

Star's apartment reminds me of the ones I used to share with my mom. The feeling hits me like a gut punch. Following her gesture, I sit on one end of the fake suede couch. Star takes the other end. It's a weird grayish-brown, with a few darker spots marking old spills.

"Jimmy's with his dad this week," Star says. I hadn't realized she had a kid, but now I see the evidence. A blue plastic squirt gun rests on the windowsill. A small pair of tennis shoes is tucked behind the front door. A half-built LEGO construction sits next to the TV.

"I appreciate you agreeing to talk."

Starr nods, tucking her hair behind her ears as I take out my new equipment. I attach the splitter to my phone and the lavaliere mics to the splitter. After demonstrating how to clip on a mic, I set the phone between us, then take out the checklist Jonas helped me with.

"Are you okay with me recording this?" I ask.

Star nods.

"For the recording, can you just say that out loud?"

"I'm okay with being recorded," Star parrots. Even though she's about my mom's age, she looks at me like I'm the adult.

I continue to read. "If you want to take a break, or me to turn off the recorder, just say so." I glance and meet her tired eyes, lined all the way around with black. "I'm so grateful you're willing to do this."

"I just want justice for Layla. It feels like everyone's forgotten her."

"But you haven't."

"I miss her every day. Every single day." Star sighs. "Sometimes I even visit her grave and talk to her. Leave her things to show she isn't just some forgotten girl."

"Like flowers?" I still don't know what to think of the destroyed bouquet, so I don't mention it.

Star nods, then remembers to speak. "Yes. Whenever I talk about her, people just say 'Sorry for your loss.' Like I just left Layla someplace. They don't want to talk about her being murdered. But saying they're sorry doesn't mean anything. It's like writing 'Keep in touch' in a yearbook. It's just something you write." She looks at me appraisingly. "Although maybe you don't know that yet."

Her words make me think of Chloe, about how far apart we've already grown.

"How did you two meet?" I ask.

"We were in the same kindergarten class. So she's been gone longer than I actually knew her." Star sighs. "It's been seventeen years and I still think about her every day and wonder what she would have become. No one should have to be seventeen years old forever. Sometimes I wonder what she'd think of how my life turned out." Her hands start to twist. "Back then we knew everything about each other. Layla was more family than my real family. I used to say blood might be thicker than water, but water tasted better."

"What was Layla like?"

She lifts her eyes to the textured ceiling, remembering. "She had this wacky laugh. Just hearing it made people happy." A smile flits across her face. "Sometimes I dream about her laughing."

My list of questions isn't tracking with her answers, but Jonas told me I should go where the interview led me. "What did it sound like?"

"Honestly, like a cackle. It embarrassed her. Sometimes she would try to laugh different, but it sounded fake. Then she'd forget and it would burst out. And that would set me off. I remember laughing so hard it physically hurt." Star presses her hands to her belly. "Once during one of those heavy summer rainstorms, we decided to wash our hair in the driveway. We were eleven and thought it would be fun. Of course it promptly stopped raining. We were standing there with shampoo running down our necks, laughing harder than hyenas."

I smile at the image, but Star's expression has already morphed into sadness.

"We swore we'd always be friends. That after graduation we'd go to the same college and share an apartment. We were going to be bridesmaids at each other's weddings. Have daughters at the same time and name them after each other." Her sigh shakes. "Back then I was going to go to college. I was going to do so much. All of it with her. Once Layla died, I felt lost."

"I'm so sorry." I hope I sound more sincere than others have. "You guys did everything together. Including dating brothers."

"That was more their idea than ours." Star puffs out air. "They were only eleven months apart. But Danny felt every one of those months. He was always trying to be like Hunter. And Hunter was always trying to outdo him. Once I started dating Hunter, Daniel had to have the next best thing."

"Layla," I say.

"Exactly." Star nods. "He chased after her for months. He would show up at her locker with gas station flowers and a stuffed bear with I L-U-V U embroidered on the belly." She spells out the letters. "It was both over the top and meaningless. Like he actually hadn't gone to that much work. But there were times Danny could be so sad, and Layla couldn't stand to see that."

"Danny was sad?" I echo.

Star shrugs. "Both those boys could be melancholy, even though they had lots of friends, their own cars, and plenty of spending money. By themselves, they could be sweet. Get them together and it was just a series of dares. Who could drive faster, drink more, get more girls, get in more fights, cut more classes, charm their way out of more trouble. Even though Hunter had graduated, he didn't really want to grow up. Dating me meant he could still hang out with high school kids. But back then I thought he was incredibly exciting. And if that meant looking the other way sometimes, then that's what I had to do."

"I've read Danny used drugs," I venture. "Maybe even sold them."

She looks at the microphone. "I can't really speak to that. But like I said, he and Hunter were always outdoing each other."

"I read an article in *The Independent* about what happened at the Hitchenses' house the morning of Layla's funeral."

"By then, Hunter and I weren't really talking. I heard the cops brought Danny and Hunter to the funeral home before the funeral, hoping to get a reaction out of them. Nobody got down on their knees and confessed. At least, not in so many words. But an overdose might be a way of admitting you can't live with your guilt."

"Danny works for his dad now, right? That's about all I've been able to tell from googling."

"I see him around town sometimes. When I do, I go the other way. He hasn't aged well."

"And Hunter?"

Star's expression changes, like someone has drawn a curtain over her eyes. "You don't know?"

"Know what?"

"Hunter's dead. I heard his dad made sure to keep it out of the papers. Six months after Layla died, he overdosed." She presses her lips together so hard they turn white.

"I'm sorry."

"Don't be. At least not for me. Because I think he had something to do with Layla's death."

I check to make sure everything is recording. Because I know what Star says is going to be the heart of my next podcast episode. All these years, people have pointed the finger at Danny.

But who was always right beside him?

"I almost forgot," Star says as I'm packing up. She picks up a silver plastic object about the size of a shoebox from next to the TV. "I dug around and found my old camcorder. My parents gave it to me for my sixteenth birthday. Back then, if you wanted good video, you had to use one of these. I still have a tape from a party the summer before."

With colored cables, she connects the camcorder to the back of her TV. It's the boxy kind you usually see sitting on the curb with FREE taped to the front.

She presses a button, and we see teens at a pool. The picture is pretty fuzzy and there's music blasting, but still it's so weird to observe these people I've spent hours reading about. I suck in my breath as Layla walks past. Her purple bikini shows off her flat stomach.

"That's Danny," Star says as a cute blond guy in long blue trunks runs past the camera. When he reaches the pool, he leaps up, grabs his knees, and comes down shouting, "Cannonball!"

"And Hunter."

The camera mostly lingers on Hunter, another good-looking kid with sun-bleached hair, a tan, and a T-shirt with the sleeves cut off to show his muscles.

But there's plenty of footage of Layla, too. I watch her move around the pool, laughing and talking to different people, gestures so expansive they look like sign language.

Layla turns to the camera and flexes, grinning. As she's showing off, Danny grabs her around the waist. While she's kicking her long legs in protest, Hunter grabs her heels, and together they unceremoniously toss her in the pool.

Next to me, Star makes a disapproving sound. When I turn, she points at a blond sitting on the edge of the pool, her back to the camera. "That's Jenny. The one who started everything by sitting on Hunter's lap."

Star is still focused on the other girl, but my attention is caught by a guy on the edge of the screen. He only has eyes for Layla, who is climbing out of the pool. He's a lot younger-looking than the version I know, but even seventeen years ago he was an adult.

It's Officer Balboa.

CHAPTER TWENTY-FOUR

SOMEONE TO BLAME
Thursday, September 24

THE WHOLE TIME I was with Star, my attention was fracturing. One part listening to her. Another readying my next question. And another part taking the thousand-foot view, trying to figure out what the overarching story of the episode would be.

Once I'm home, I click on a free online artificial intelligence program Jonas recommended to start generating a transcript of my conversation with Star. I also check my e-mails and DMs. Every day I've been getting one or two. The count for the first podcast is up to nearly eighteen hundred.

"This was definitely done by someone in the area. I
live in Firview and 75% of the people that live here

wouldn't be able to find Bettinger Butte, never mind someone from out of town."

"I was looking for something to listen to. Wow—what an interesting story. I can't wait to learn more."

Feeling a glow of pride, I come downstairs and help Gretchen make dinner. The kids are in the living room watching *Arthur*.

"How's school going?" she asks as she dices an onion and I cut potatoes into chunks. "The kids are always so chatty at dinner, it's hard to have a real conversation."

"It's okay," I say. "Thank you for asking." I know I'm treating her like a stranger, but it seems safer that way.

"Every time I see you, you always seem to be working hard on something." She sweeps the onions into a pan and adds a glug of olive oil.

"We have to pick a senior passion project that lasts the whole year. I'm working on a podcast."

While I'm talking, her head swivels toward the living room, where the kids are starting to argue. "Just let us know if you need any help." When Sequoia shrieks, Gretchen starts toward them. "Can you stir the onion and add the Better Than Beef?"

"Sure." After I add the potatoes to the boiling water, I cut open the package of fake hamburger and add it to the sizzling onion. As the major meltdown in the living room continues, I consult the stained recipe and start adding the other ingredients. I never appreciated my mom's cooking until I didn't have it.

I try to keep thoughts of my mom walled off, but now I can feel the wall crumbling. I miss her so much. She always said we were a team. She was happiest when people asked if we were sisters. If I could talk to her, I would tell her about Jonas and his accident.

I googled him after he told me what happened. Last year Jonas was considered one of the state's top five pitching prospects, even though he was only a junior. The *Firview Times* said there was talk of "major college interest." That must be gone now. Of course, it pales in comparison with Suzie's death, but still.

If I were Alice, would I see Jonas as a killer, too?

Are Star's accusations of the Hitchens brothers any more logical? Or is it simply the human need to find someone to blame?

If my mom were here, I could discuss that with her. She loved *Dead, Deader, Deadest*, too, and would immediately understand why I had to do the podcast.

What had it been like for Layla's friends and family? One day she was there, and the next she was gone. I know what that's like. Just like I know that the stages of grief— denial, anger, bargaining, acceptance, or whatever—don't come in a neat order. Sometimes they return over and over, like waves that alternate between pulling you under and spitting you back onto the shore.

By the time Gretchen returns, the shepherd's pie filling is ready and I'm mashing the potatoes to go on top.

"Thank you so much, Piper. I don't know what I would have done without you." She puts her hand over her heart.

Gretchen's not bad. She's just not my mom.

CHAPTER TWENTY-FIVE

START AT THE END AND WORK BACKWARD

Thursday, September 24

ONCE I'M BACK UPSTAIRS, I text Jonas.

"The transcription is done. I'm going to start logging my tape."

He texts back right away. "Okay. Let me know when you're done."

I print out the transcript, then put on my earbuds. I read along while simultaneously listening to our conversation. The transcript doesn't have commas or periods, and sometimes it's typed the wrong word. But since I was there for the real thing, it's not too confusing.

As I listen, I briefly outline the basics of what we said, with time stamps.

0:00 Recording starts, small talk. Star agrees to taping.

0:22 People sorry for loss

0:31 How S/L met

As I scribble, I wonder how best to shape it into a podcast. The scripts for my first two podcasts weren't easy, but I still had complete control. I could tell the facts in an order that made the most sense.

Now I'm limited to what Star said—not what I wished she'd said or imaginary answers to questions I wish I'd asked. But I guess it's not that much different from having to rely on articles that didn't raise the points I wish they had.

When I finish, I text Jonas. "I'm done logging." And then I put on lip gloss and make sure there's nothing weird or embarrassing in the background.

He answers with a video call. "Okay. Now the real work begins. How many minutes is it?"

"Fifty-seven and some change."

He whistles. "You're going to have to cut a lot."

"I might let this episode run a little longer. Star said a lot of interesting things. But there's one thing she didn't talk about. I don't know if she even realized it was strange. And it speaks to what you said."

"What?" Jonas leans closer to the screen.

"She showed me a video of this pool party. It was weird seeing Layla and Danny and Hunter in three dimensions, talking and laughing. It made them more real. But someone else was there." I pause for effect. "Officer Balboa."

His mouth opens. "Whoa."

"He was a lot younger, obviously, but still an adult. Like you said. An adult at a pool party where everyone else is in high school."

"You probably don't know this, but Officer Balboa got married over the summer to this girl, Sarah Pierce. She lives on my block. She's only two years older than us, and it's his fourth marriage. I guess a leopard never changes its spots."

I make a face. "Or not a leopard, but whatever the male version of a cougar is. And he's got a gut."

Jonas shrugs. "And a uniform. Maybe some girls like that."

I shake my head to clear the thought. "I guess I should just focus on turning this interview into a podcast. Right now it's kind of a mess. There were so many tangents and asides."

"Your first step is going to be to make a copy," Jonas says. "That way, even if you mess up, it's not permanent. Then use your notes to figure out what you know for sure you can cut."

"Okay."

"And here's a trick I didn't figure out for a while. Don't start off by cutting out things from the beginning. If you do that, all the other time stamps become inaccurate. Instead, start at the end and work backward."

I nod. "That's smart."

"And don't waste your time cutting out every little in-breath. Focus on taking out or reordering entire sections to tell a better story. And then when it feels like you've done as much as you can, print out a new transcript. And start all over again." He smiles. "And feel free to call me if you have questions."

After saying goodbye, I start in. At first I'm tentative. Everything seems important. But I still have almost forty minutes of recording left. That's way too much.

I keep winnowing, cutting a half sentence here, a paragraph there. Eventually I follow the final tip Jonas gave me and take scissors to what's left, cutting it into chunks. Some are nearly a full page long, others just a sentence. After laying them on my bedroom floor, I shuffle the pieces around until they make sense. Finally I tape everything together.

Then I take all my notes, pages, and strips of paper and digitally edit my interview with Star again. When I listen to what I've done, it's better. It's not perfect, but better. I make notes on what still isn't working, and edit it some more. I record voice-overs for places where I have to put myself in the story, to explain things that otherwise won't make sense, or to reiterate key details.

It's nearly two in the morning, but I finally have a solid draft of episode 4: "The Friend."

CHAPTER TWENTY-SIX

PARTIAL TRANSCRIPT OF EPISODE 4 OF *WHO KILLED LAYLA TRELLO?*: "THE FRIEND"

Air date: September 27

STAR: LAYLA BROKE ME out of my shell and I kept her impulsiveness in check.

Piper: Impulsiveness?

Star: Layla was always straining against the leash, even when it choked her. Maybe *especially* when it choked her.

Piper: What do you mean?

Star: Her parents expected her to be perfect, but Layla liked to be a little wild. Occasionally a lot wild. Like this party. We were going to go together and then come back to my house. She hadn't told her parents about the party, only that she was going to sleep over at my house. But then I got sick. When she called me that night, I'd already been asleep for hours. It was way past midnight. Two things were clear: she was messed up, and she was mad at Hunter.

Piper voice-over: Star is talking about Hunter Hitchens, Star's boyfriend at the time. Hunter was the older brother of Layla's boyfriend, Danny.

Star: Layla said she'd caught Hunter with this girl, Jenny, on his lap. Which actually wasn't a big surprise. She had been interested in him for a while and Hunter wasn't exactly the faithful type. Once Jenny heard I was sick, she must have figured it was her chance. I told Layla to let it go, but she said she was going to go tell Hunter off.

Piper: Do you think she did?

Star: I do. I think that's what got her killed, or at least led to it. It has to have been one of them. Hunter or Danny. Danny's story was that they argued and Layla decided to walk home. But that never made sense. Messed up or not, she wouldn't do that. It was over three miles. When I tried to ask Hunter about it, I could tell he was lying.

Piper: But why kill Layla for being upset about Hunter kissing another girl? That's a big overreaction.

Star: Hunter was impulsive. So was Danny. And when they were angry, they liked to break things. I'm sure all three of them were off their faces. Maybe Hunter or both of them were just trying to scare her into being quiet. All I know is Layla said she was going to call out Hunter, and that's the last time I ever talked to her.

Piper: But where would they have gotten the gun?

Star: Lots of people own guns around here. Even my parents had a handgun. Hunter had told me their dad owned a couple. Or maybe they found it at the house where the party was being held.

Piper: So after Layla disappeared, what happened between you and Hunter?

Star: At first, when she was just missing, I was crying on his shoulder. I didn't even care about that stupid girl he'd kissed. When they found Layla's broken phone, I told myself that explained why she hadn't contacted me. Maybe she was still alive, just in trouble. But whenever I talked to Hunter about that night, it felt like there were holes in his story. When I kept asking, he got mad. So I stopped seeing him, or maybe he stopped seeing me. After Layla's body was found, there were rumors that Rich Hitchens pulled strings to make sure his boys weren't looked at too closely. A few months before, he'd already made sure an earlier assault charge went away. So maybe they did it again.

Piper voice-over: Star's referring to an assault case the previous May involving both Hitchens boys. They were arrested, but the charges were dropped after the victim didn't show up in court.

Piper: But murder? That's a lot bigger than having a fight with a kid in a parking lot.

Star: You think so? They fractured that kid's skull.

Piper voice-over: Star also told me something that never made the papers. Hunter Hitchens died six months after Layla's murder, from what sounds like a drug overdose.

Star: I just want to know the truth. Layla would have been cautious around a stranger. But I think she knew the person who killed her. Trusted them. And that trust got her killed.

Piper voice-over: Contemporary reports said there were over a hundred people at the party. I would love to hear from anyone who was there. It's been nearly two decades. Maybe back then you kept quiet to protect someone and now you don't need to. Maybe you saw something but never told anyone. Maybe Layla shared a secret with you that you promised to never tell, but breaking your silence now might help find her killer.

CHAPTER TWENTY-SEVEN

NOT BECAUSE SHE KILLED HER
Tuesday, September 29

Even without any more Krispy Kremes, Creative Writing continues to be my favorite class. A few days ago, Mrs. Wharton had us write from the point of view of an inanimate object—the sights, sounds, hopes, and fears it might have. I chose an elevator. I described its thoughts about various passengers, how it saw itself as providing an important function.

The class is also improving my podcast. Mrs. Wharton has gotten me thinking about how to use strong verbs. How to show instead of tell. How and when to reveal information.

Today I'm engrossed in writing a two-page story about an event that happens in sixty seconds. Tomorrow we'll write its companion: a two-page story that covers sixty years. When the bell rings, I jump.

As we gather our things, Mrs. Wharton says, "Stay for a second, Piper?"

Jonas looks at me, his eyebrows pulling together. I lift my shoulders in a shrug.

She sits on a corner of her desk, one leg moving like a pendulum. After everyone leaves, she says, "Ms. Kernow told me about your senior passion project. I listened to everything you've put out so far. I think I might be able to help you with it."

Mrs. Wharton has talked about things she likes to do—ski, go to concerts, travel—but I've never heard her mention podcasts.

"You know how to podcast?"

"No." She lowers her voice. "But I actually went to school with Layla Trello. She was a year older than me, so I didn't know her that well." She bites her lip, then adds, "But I was at the party. The one she disappeared from."

"Wow!" My pulse speeds up. Every day I get DMs and e-mails, but mostly they just repeat rumors. No one who was there has agreed to be interviewed for the podcast. "Can I interview you? I could do it over lunch."

"We can talk, but not on tape and you can't use my name. I'm a professional now. I don't need anyone in admin thinking of me as some party girl."

"Were you?" I ask. "A party girl?"

"I was trying." With a secret smile, she shakes her head, her eyes unfocused. "That night I was wearing this stupid 'sexy'"—she makes air quotes—"gangster costume." She interrupts herself. "Why do costumes for girls always have to be sexy? Sexy cowgirl, sexy nurse, sexy witch..."

I've wondered the same thing myself. "Besides conforming to gender stereotypes, it's probably cheaper. They don't have to use as much fabric."

Her laugh is short and staccato. "Ha! You're probably right. There certainly wasn't a lot of fabric in mine. Black short-shorts, black cropped shirt, fingerless gloves with silver studs on the back, and this ridiculous pleather thigh holster for a silver plastic gun. I wore it with some black Doc Martens. I thought I looked so cool."

When Jonas asks me during free period what Mrs. Wharton wanted, I don't tell the whole truth. "She told me she'd been listening to the podcast."

"Wow. A teacher. Did that feel weird?"

"A little." More kids have asked me about it, but this is the first time an adult has.

I spend the morning pretending to take notes in various classes while really making a list of questions. At lunch, I find Mrs. Wharton eating a take-out salad.

She's the first to ask a question. "So, Piper, who do you think did it?" She loads up her fork.

"I don't know enough to know yet."

She balances a crouton on top of the forkful.

"I've heard rumors that Star ended up going to the party to confront Hunter."

I blink. "Did you see her?"

"No. But what if she was mad enough to bring a gun with her?" Mrs. Wharton points the tines of her plastic fork at me. "And she told you that her parents had one."

I try to think it through. "Even if she did, I don't see how that scenario ends with Layla dead. She was Star's best friend."

"But Star probably didn't know how to handle a gun. Maybe Layla tried to stop her from going after Hunter. What if there was some kind of terrible accident?" She chews thoughtfully. "And Star was really broken up afterward."

"But if it was an accident, why not go to the police?"

Mrs. Wharton makes a scoffing sound. "And ruin her life forever? Star probably thought if she could hide the body, no one would ever find out."

Star is so sad, even now. But it's because she loved Layla. Not because she killed her. Right? Besides, there are other suspects.

"Star showed me this video of a pool party she had a few months before Layla died. And guess who else was there?"

Her eyes widen and she stops chewing. "Who?"

"Officer Balboa! At a high school party."

Mrs. Wharton takes another bite and chews thoughtfully. "Damon might have had a reason for spending time with Layla." I expect her to talk about Officer Balboa's string of young wives, but instead she lowers her voice to a whisper. "I've heard Layla was his CI."

"CI?" I echo.

"Confidential informant. That year, several kids ended up being expelled for drug dealing. One even got tried as an adult and went to prison."

Any of them might have wanted to hurt Layla. "What was the person's name? The one who went to prison?" I say the word *prison* as if it holds no weight for me.

"It was so long ago." Mrs. Wharton spears a cherry tomato. "I don't remember any details."

"Why would Layla do that? What would she get out of it?"

"Officer Balboa might have looked the other way on a few things involving the Hitchens brothers. And he might have thought it was worth catching some smaller fish if you know the bigger ones will just slither out of the net no matter how tight it is." She bites the tomato with her perfect white teeth.

"Do you mean Danny and Hunter?"

"People said those boys were untouchable."

"Everyone seems to think one or both of them killed Layla," I say. "But why would they kill her if she was the one protecting them?"

"They were both hot-tempered. Always getting into trouble." She half smiles. "Actually, in high school, those qualities can seem attractive, but they don't work so well when you're an adult. Although I guess Hunter never got to be one. But when you're eighteen, you can look gorgeous even if you're drinking, using drugs, and not getting your beauty rest. It's like nature offsets all your bad habits, probably in an effort to let you procreate. I was so young I thought it was cool that the boys had their own cars. And nice cars, too. I didn't realize everything just got handed to them."

"How well did you know them?"

"Danny was a year older than me, and Hunter was two. Danny used to flirt with me sometimes, but I don't think Hunter even saw me. Two years is an eternity when you're that age." Mrs. Wharton turns serious. "But there's one thing about the party you should know. At one point, I looked out the front window and saw Layla outside arguing with Hunter."

The hair rises on my arms. "What kind of argument? Physical?"

She raises one shoulder. "Just yelling. Waving their arms around."

"Star said Layla was going to confront Hunter. But Danny told the paper that he was the one Layla argued with."

"Maybe Danny was just trying to confuse the issue. Those two always had each other's backs."

I remember what Star said. "But then Hunter OD'ed."

"That might be why the case went cold. Because the cops knew the guy who did it was dead. No point in dragging the rest of the family through that." Mrs. Wharton snaps the lid back on her salad bowl and puts it in the trash. "In their minds, it might even have been justice."

CHAPTER TWENTY-EIGHT

TIGHT-KNIT
Wednesday, September 30

RECORDING STAR WAS ONE thing. She was eager to talk about Layla. And because I spend nearly an hour with her every weekday, I felt comfortable around Mrs. Wharton. But it's hard to imagine it being the same with Officer Balboa, especially once I start asking questions about the exact nature of his relationship to Layla.

I've had some experience with cops. Lots of them came into the Over Easy. Maybe that's why they took what happened with my mom so personally. I know that cops like to sit with their backs against the wall. They're always alert, paying particular attention to hands. They're not chatty. The rare times they joke, the humor is as dark and bitter as a pot of coffee forgotten on the burner.

And while some are happy to accept a free meal, others will insist on paying—and leave an excellent tip.

For a few days, I debate how to approach Officer Balboa. I'm guessing he won't want to be taped. Google says that in Oregon, it's legal to record your phone conversations, but in-person conversations require everyone's consent. But if I call him, he'll just suggest we meet in his office. Even if he does agree to taping, once I mention Layla, that might end the interview. But what if I approach it sideways?

Wednesday, I skip the cafeteria during lunch period and head to his office. When I peep through the half-open door, he's reading the *Firview Times*. A partially eaten sub rests on top of a paper bag.

When I knock on the door frame, Officer Balboa gets to his feet. "Come in."

At my old school, the resource officer dressed in street clothes. But Officer Balboa is in full uniform, navy blue so dark it's almost black. He's got one of those square bodies that could be made of muscle, fat, or both. On his left hip is a Taser and on his right, a gun.

"I'm Piper Gray."

He gives me a look up and down, taking in my white polyester shirt with stylized flowers, my gray pants with a fly that buttons on the outside. "I know who you are."

"Oh." I feel off-balance. Does he know about my mom? Or has he listened to the podcast?

"I make it a point to know every student." He sits and gestures for me to take the chair facing his desk. "We're a tight-knit community."

I forge ahead. "I was wondering if I could interview you for a few minutes. I'm doing a podcast for my senior passion project, and I'm interesting in learning more about North's antidrug program."

None of this is technically a lie.

"Antidrug, huh?" he echoes, and by the way he says it, I know he knows about my mom. "Good choice. Do you want to do that now? Or do I need to prepare something?"

"Now would be great." The last thing I want is for Officer Balboa to be prepared.

"What's all this for?" he asks as I set everything up on top of his desk.

"A podcast is just sound. For the best quality, we each need to wear a mic." I hand him his lavaliere mic and then attach my own. Following my lead, he clips his between two buttons of his crisp uniform shirt.

"Do I sound all right?" His words are both over-enunciated and too loud.

"You can just speak naturally." I keep my tone casual. "And you're okay with me recording this?"

"Of course. Anything to get the word out about our program."

I look down at my notes. "Today I'm speaking with Officer Balboa, the antidrug officer at North High in

Firview, Oregon." As I speak, he shapes his lips into a smile. "So Officer Balboa, I understand you've worked here a long time."

"That is correct. It's been over twenty years." He's still speaking formally. "To be honest, it's not always easy. It has to be your passion." He taps the left side of his broad chest. "Your heart. If it's just a job, the kids will know it."

"And it's called the DARE program?"

"It used to be DARE. Drug Abuse Resistance Education. Now it's all about keeping it REAL: Refuse, Explain, Avoid, and Leave. If I can prevent just one student from using opioids or other drugs, then it's a success."

"So what else has changed over time, besides the name?"

"Our original curriculum was more lecture-based. Now it's student-centered. We come together in a non-adversarial way so we can learn from one another." He leans forward. "In practical terms, I'm here to give students a friendly ear so they can stop using drugs or stay away from them altogether. I want you kids to look at me as an older brother who's got your best interests at heart. So remember, Piper, if you ever have a problem or a question, you can always come see me."

I wish I was recording video. Because my MP3 file won't capture the creepy vibe he's giving off.

I keep my expression the same. "When you started here, was drug use much of a problem?"

"Oh, for sure." To my relief, Officer Balboa sits back. "Fifteen, twenty years ago there wasn't as much awareness. Kids were starting to use and even sell their parents' old painkillers, not understanding they were setting themselves up for a lifelong addiction. That is, if they didn't overdose. Back then, kids had this idea that if it was a prescription drug, that meant it couldn't hurt them."

Thoughts of my mom intrude. Had she believed what she was doing was safe?

I say, "The reason I've been thinking about that time is because I recently walked through Skyline Cemetery."

Looking a bit confused, Office Balboa nods.

"One grave caught my eye. It belonged to this girl named Layla Trello. I googled and found out she'd been a student here. And that she was murdered. Did you know her?"

Officer Balboa doesn't ask me who Layla was. His memory doesn't need any prodding. "Poor girl." He shakes his head, his mouth turning down at the corners.

"When I read about it, it seemed like some people thought Layla's death might have had something to do with drugs. They said her boyfriend sold them."

"There were rumors to that effect," he says carefully.

"I also heard that Layla was your CI. Confidential informant."

His eyes widen in surprise. "Who told you that? That's not true."

"The rumor was that information she provided led to

several students being expelled, and at least one being sent to prison."

"That is a complete load of—of hooey." He waves one hand. "I mean, I talked to Layla from time to time, but she certainly didn't work for me."

An idea blooms inside my chest. "Were you at the party? The one she disappeared from?"

He makes a scoffing noise. "No. You can be sure I would have put a stop to any drinking or drug use if I was."

I don't mention that I have seen him on a video at a different party. But it's true that I hadn't seen even a single beer bottle among the crowd at the pool.

"I guess there's so little information to go on that people must have started making up their own answers." I pause. "What do you think happened to her?"

"Layla was always friendly to everyone." Officer Balboa sighs. "Maybe someone assumed that friendliness meant more than it did. And when they realized they'd made a mistake, they thought: *She can never tell anyone what I've done.* That's what I believe."

The hairs raise on my arms. Could Office Balboa be talking about himself? I remember the way he looked at her in Star's video. I think of that girl, Sarah, the one Jonas told me he married a few months ago.

He's still speaking. "When I heard a female cadaver had been found, I knew right away it was her. I responded to the scene and made a positive identification." He sighs.

"So you were at Gilkey Creek?" An idea teases me, but I can't pin it down.

"Yes. I helped remove the body."

A piece of the idea falls into place. "I know police look at shoeprints and other evidence from the scene. How can they sort out what the killer left from what the person who found her or the first responders did?"

"That's an excellent question, Piper." He nods appreciatively. "The crime scene techs gather elimination samples from everyone who had lawful access to the scene, and of course the investigators wear bunny suits, booties, and gloves. So they got samples from me, to help them tell the good guys from the bad guys."

But I can't help thinking: What if a good guy *was* the bad guy?

Was there a reason Officer Balboa responded so quickly?

CHAPTER TWENTY-NINE

SWEAT, CIGARETTES, AND MOTHBALLS

Saturday, October 3

I'VE NEVER BEEN TO Firview Fair Value before, but when I step inside the thrift store the smell is deeply familiar. It's a mix of wool, perfume, and fabric softener, with touches of sweat, cigarettes, and mothballs. Taking an appreciative sniff, I scan the space, trying to figure out where to start. Probably not kitchen wares or furniture or shoes. Clothing for sure, but it's possible the knickknack aisles could have something cool or interesting. Fair Value is about the size of a small grocery store, which is what I think the space might have been originally.

"Hey, Piper!" Jonas says from behind me.

I turn with a smile. "Ready for your big adventure?" For once I'll be the expert.

He nods. "So where do we start?"

"How about men's clothes?" I suggest. "They're less likely to be picked over."

We start with the suits while I tell Jonas about how Officer Balboa reacted to Mrs. Wharton's rumor.

"He said she wasn't a confidential informant," I say, rapidly sliding hangers from right to left. Most of the jackets are either weird (but not weird enough to be cool), or so worn the elbows are shiny. "But I'm not sure I believe him. It didn't feel like he was one hundred percent honest with me."

"I don't think Officer Balboa is one hundred percent honest with anyone," Jonas says. "On the other hand, Layla seems like she was more of a party girl than a narc."

"But by definition, if she was a confidential informant, it would be secret. Maybe even still. Especially if her informing on people led to her being killed. The police wouldn't want information on that getting out. And there's more." I explain about how Officer Balboa responding to the call about her body could have muddied the evidence.

Jonas makes a face. "Balboa might be a creeper—but a killer? I can't really buy that." He pauses on a bright blue suit improbably patterned with hundreds of Batman logos.

With my hand, I shield my eyes from the garish pattern. "Please tell me you're not going to get that." Then I pull out the sleeve of a navy blue suit with a subtle pinstripe. "See how they rounded the corner on the cuff just a little bit? It's to keep it from wearing out prematurely. That's a sign of higher quality." I check the label at the neck. "One hundred percent wool. That doesn't necessarily mean it's old, but if it were a blend, it's definitely a sign that it's newer."

"How'd you learn all this stuff?" Jonas asks.

"My mom." I smile at my many memories of us unearthing amazing finds. "If you shop used, you can buy literally ten times as much clothing for your money. And you won't look like everyone else." I flip up the jacket's tag. "And look. Made in the US. That's another sign this suit is at least forty years old. And it's only seven-ninety-nine. A steal."

"Yeah, but I think you are overlooking something, Piper. It's huge." Jonas pulls the rest of the jacket free. It's nearly a yard across the chest. "It would never fit me."

He's right.

"I got so caught up in the details I forgot to look at the big picture." My own words hit home. Am I forgetting to look at the big picture?

We keep talking and looking. Eventually he follows me as I check the women's clothes. I lean over a rack and pull out an aqua blouse. My fingers run over the fabric as I examine it. The color is good, the fabric still soft and supple, but the self-bow dates it to the early eighties. I like my retro to be a little more retro. I put it back.

In the shoe section, Jonas find a pair of old-fashioned roller skates in his size. They are black with blue wheels.

"Do you think you can"—I start and then stop. We've still never directly talked about what it's like to have only one real leg. I get the feeling Jonas doesn't want to draw any attention to it.

"If I use my good leg for pushing, I think it might work."

We end up spending a couple of hours looking at the weird and the wild. When we leave, I have a leopard-print blouse, a corduroy jacket in a beautiful shade of midnight blue, a wide silver bracelet made of hammered metal, and tortoiseshell cat-eye sunglasses. Jonas gets a porkpie hat and a T-shirt with a faded Rolling Stones logo. And the roller skates.

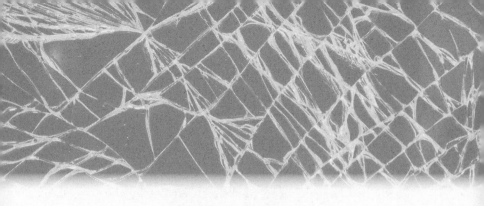

CHAPTER THIRTY

PARTIAL TRANSCRIPT OF EPISODE 5 OF *WHO KILLED LAYLA TRELLO?*: "THE RUMORS"
Air date: October 4

IN THE COURSE OF working on this podcast, I've read every article about Layla's case online or on microfiche.

I've also spent hours online searching for photos of Layla, finding them in unlikely places, like on sports blogs and Pinterest. Layla's Facebook page is still live, and I've read every comment and public message.

With few facts, monsters were conjured and fingers were pointed. People stayed home and got on the internet. Everyone has an opinion, the saying goes, but now they had an opinion, a computer, and a way to share their suspicions. So rumors spread.

Today we're going to examine several of those rumors.

Could Layla have been the victim of a serial killer? I've tried to examine any unsolved murders of women within a hundred-mile radius and in a five-year time span bracketing Layla's murder. I looked for patterns. Parallels. But I couldn't find any. One woman was strangled, another stabbed. One woman's body had been reduced to skeletal remains by the time she was found, so authorities aren't sure of her cause of death. Only one woman was shot, her body found in her burning car. But while those murders are still unsolved, they did have one thing in common. They were all the kind of woman who, sadly, often makes the perfect victim. And I don't mean the perfect victim like we've talked about from the media's point of view: young, white, photogenic. No, I'm speaking of those who would make a perfect victim from a killer's point of view: homeless, drug-addicted, and/or sex workers. The kind of women who when they disappear, no one even notices they are missing.

But Layla was definitely missed.

There was another rumor that was almost the flip side of the first—that Layla had been killed by someone from the wrong side of the tracks, someone who was down and out, mentally ill, homeless, or drug addicted. Firview residents didn't want to think that a "nice middle-class person" could do something so horrible. But there's no reason someone down on their luck would want to harm a girl at a party in a suburban neighborhood. You are much more likely to be killed by someone who knows you than by a stranger.

One person who knew Layla well was Hunter Hitchens.

Layla had told her best friend, Star, on the phone that she was going to confront Hunter about him kissing another girl. I have since spoken to an anonymous witness who told me they saw Layla and Hunter arguing on the front lawn. Danny bore the brunt of the suspicions, but what if the killer was actually his brother? If that's true, his overdose a few months later might have been a suicide and could seem logical.

What makes Layla's case so uniquely difficult is that for nearly two weeks, it wasn't a murder case. It was a missing person's case. It's possible police didn't take it as seriously as they could have. They may have thought Layla had run away or run off with some guy. By the time authorities learned the truth, the case was going cold.

Time is not on the authorities' side. Evidence degrades or gets lost. Witnesses move away. People's memories get foggy.

But time can also be an ally. In fact, changes in technology and human relationships can make it possible to use that passage of time to our advantage.

For example, every day, new fingerprints and DNA profiles are added to federal databases. If the offender is arrested on unrelated charges, once their information is entered, then a cold case can suddenly turn hot.

Since Layla was stripped of her clothing, there was nothing that might have yielded fingerprints. In fact, that might have been the reason her belongings were missing. Some people theorized the reason Layla's body was dumped in water was to try to wash off DNA.

When investigators recover DNA from a murder victim, it's not always from a sexual assault. There's also something called trace DNA, which is what it sounds like: a tiny amount of DNA, like skin cells, left behind by the assailant. Did Layla struggle with her killer? In the autopsy, they would have cleaned under her fingernails, hoping to find a fragment of her killer's skin. But if they did find anything, that information was never made public. And even finding DNA won't solve a case, not if there is no match in the database. Did they ask Danny and other people at the party for DNA samples? I can't find any reports that they did. But then again Danny was Layla's boyfriend. Finding his DNA on her wouldn't have been a red flag.

Speaking of DNA, one of the first cops on the scene told me that because he helped move Layla's body from the creek bank, he later provided authorities with elimination samples. These samples help investigators know what evidence is innocuous. For example, if this officer touched Layla's body with ungloved hands, he could've left DNA behind. It's the same reason detectives would have gotten the shoeprints of everyone at the scene.

The thing is, this officer already knew Layla because he worked at her school. Some claim she may have passed on information to him, others just say that they spent time together. I'm not going to use his name because, like I said, these are only rumors. I will say that earlier this year, this officer married his fourth wife, a girl who graduated from

North High just two years ago. And he told me that Layla was friendly to everyone, and he felt that friendliness could have been misinterpreted.

Another way time may work to the investigators' advantage is that people can grow apart. Maybe years ago, someone was friends with the killer, but now they aren't. Or people may get tired of living with guilt. Also, many of those who may have had knowledge of the case were just kids at the time. They've had a chance to mature, and the things that influenced them back in the day may no longer hold the same force. A fourth possibility is that over time the perpetrator might have confided in others—others who now might be willing to talk.

Since I started this podcast, I've heard from so many people who knew Layla, or who were at the party. A lot of people have told me they believe the Hitchens brothers were never seriously considered as suspects, even though they deserved to be. What's interesting is the nearly complete silence about them in outlets such as the *Firview Times*. Could that have anything to do with the copious amount of newspaper advertising Hitchens Auto Group does?

CHAPTER THIRTY-ONE

EVERYONE LIKES TO BE
LOOKED AT

Wednesday, October 7

ON MY WAY TO school, I check out the latest messages about the podcast. It's up to 2,500 listeners now.

> "Did you know Layla's boyfriend sold drugs? I know that for a fact, because I bought some from him back in the day."

That's followed by several compliments. By the time I open the last message, I'm feeling pretty proud of myself.

> "You can't bring Layla back from the dead. You need to watch yourself."

That last one gives me pause. It's from someone named Ammon Mal. When I click on it, the Facebook account doesn't exist. It's the fourth threatening warning I've received.

Is it just one person being a wiseass, hiding behind a fake name, trying to scare me? Or is it a real threat?

When I google the name, it turns out *Ammon* can mean "secret or hidden," and *Mal* means "bad." I decide it's just a stupid troll. Because I can't stop now, not when I feel like I am finally learning things. Maybe Danny or Hunter had nothing to do with Layla's death, or maybe they worked together, or maybe Hunter let everyone point fingers at Danny when he was secretly the one who did it. Maybe the police never caught the killer because he was one of their own.

It could even be somebody random. A newspaper delivery guy. Some man who happened to be driving by and offered Layla a ride. My thoughts collide and tangle as I walk into Mrs. Wharton's class.

The fifty minutes pass by in a blur. As we're walking out of class, Jonas asks, "Do you know Mrs. Nelson?"

I remember the short woman from the assembly, the one wearing turquoise reading glasses on a pink lanyard. "The lady who oversees the yearbook?"

He nods. "She's got this storage closet filled with boxes, one for each yearbook. They go back forever. There might be photos of Layla you haven't seen."

Excitement floods my veins. "That's a great idea." Why hadn't I thought about the yearbook? Is there anything else obvious that I'm overlooking?

At lunch, Jonas meets me at Mrs. Nelson's classroom door and we walk in together. "This is Piper Gray," he says. "The one with that podcast about Layla Trello."

Mrs. Nelson tilts her head. "When I heard her name in the hall the other day, I thought I was imagining it. Right after she died, Layla was all anyone at school talked about, but now she's forgotten. Or at least she had been."

"I want to shine a fresh light on what happened," I say.

Mrs. Nelson's laugh is a bark. "When you do that, you end up surprising roaches, spiders, and other things that live in the darkness. And they don't like the light."

"Jonas told me about your yearbook boxes. Could I look through the ones for the years Layla was here?"

Mrs. Nelson opens the door to a large closet filled with bankers boxes stacked higher than our heads. "Before I retire, I need to decide what to do with these. It doesn't feel right to have maintenance just haul them to the trash."

Each box is scribbled with a year, but they aren't in any order, so we have to dig. Dust soon fills the air, but eventually we find the four boxes covering Layla's time.

When I lift the lid of the box for her senior year, it releases the scents of a used bookstore: dust, mildew, and slowly decaying paper. The finished annual sits on a jumble of photos. Its first two pages are dedicated to Layla, with the dates of her birth and death, pictures of her running, and a banner across the top: "Gone but Not Forgotten."

"For most students," Mrs. Nelson says, "Layla's was the first death they'd ever experienced."

"What was she like as a person?" I ask.

"Popular and friendly. A solid student. She had some trouble sitting still. If she hadn't died I might not remember her as well as I do. Her death cast a shadow over the rest of the year."

"Some people who've messaged me say she was a flirt," I venture.

"Layla had just figured out everyone likes to be looked at. So she looked at people, really looked, and they looked right back."

As Mrs. Nelson speaks, I page back to the *H*s, then show Jonas. "This is Danny." Although he probably doesn't look like a surfer dude anymore.

Jonas's mouth thins. "One of the people your podcast has pointed the finger at."

"I just talk about what other people think might have happened. Like Star Stoddard. She was Star Munroe back then." I find her picture. "She believes it was Danny or Hunter or maybe both of them."

He gives his head a little shake. "And you just let her put that out there."

"Because I don't know what the truth is. That's why I'm asking people to share information."

Mrs. Nelson is looking back and forth between us like we're a tennis match. "Well, Piper, if you were in my class, I would tell you that good journalism is guided by five values." She ticks them off on her fingers. "We must be truthful, objective, fair, diligent, and accountable." Then she throws her hands up in the air. "That's all well and good, but enough time has passed that it's difficult to know what the truth is. So your podcast has to rely on people's memories. And over time, we edit our memories, sometimes unconsciously."

"And you can't say Star's view is objective," Jonas says. "Layla was her best friend."

I cross my arms. "The only people who know something about what happened are people with a stake in the outcome."

"And now you have a stake, too," Mrs. Nelson says. "But when you stand to benefit, you have to exercise caution."

I laugh. "I'm good on that one. I'm just doing this for school credit."

She raises a skeptical eyebrow. "But won't more salacious details get more listeners? And listeners are a form of currency."

"I don't need to make stuff up," I say, stung. "Real life is shocking enough all by itself."

Mrs. Nelson doesn't back down. "Still, you must be prepared to accept criticism. And consequences. Because you're young, you think seventeen years ago is ancient history. But it's no time at all." Her eyes, caught in a net of wrinkles, regard me steadily. "I teach the principle of harm limitation. You need to weigh the negative consequences of any disclosure."

A pit opens in my stomach. "Are you talking about Officer Balboa?"

"He's a buffoon. Always so eager to act like he's one of you. Teachers and school personnel aren't your friends. We're your mentors." Mrs. Nelson purses her lips in distaste. "But rumors aren't facts. A good journalist doesn't pander to lurid curiosity."

While we've been talking, Jonas has been looking at the photos that intersperse the yearbook headshots. Football players listening to their coach. A wrestler grimacing as he puts his opponent in a headlock. A girl blowing a bubble nearly as big as her head. A guy onstage wearing a glued-on beard that looks like an animal pelt.

"What was Mrs. Wharton's name back then?" I ask Mrs. Nelson. "She said she was a junior when Layla was killed."

"Fugate," Mrs. Nelson says.

Jonas flips to the Fs, then taps his finger on her photo. Virginia Fugate. She looks less finished, more forgettable.

After paging through the rest of the annual, we look

through the photos that didn't make the cut. It's easy to see why most weren't chosen. Many are out of focus, or lack a focal point.

Boys chasing after a loose basketball. A girl laughing, her hands a blur but the expression so genuine I automatically smile back.

"Wait," I say. "That's Layla."

"So it is." Mrs. Nelson offers it to me. "Do you want it?"

I take it while Jonas finishes thumbing through the rest of the stack. He's about to dump them all back in the sagging cardboard box when my gaze snags on Layla in the background of another photo. Her face is in profile. Her hand is on a blond guy's shoulder, leaning in to whisper in his ear. The two of them are as close as can be.

"Who is that?" Jonas asks. "Is it Danny?"

Mrs. Nelson squints through her reading glasses. "I think it's Hunter."

CHAPTER THIRTY-TWO

A GIRL IS DEAD
Wednesday, October 7

WHEN I LEAVE MRS. Nelson's classroom, my mind is racing. More and more, it seems like Hunter should have been the prime suspect, not Danny. Suddenly the crowded hall—shoulders knocking into mine, feet nearly tripping me, the sound level so loud people have to shout to be heard—is overwhelming. I still have five minutes before the bell rings. At the end of the hall, I push open the exit door and step out into the welcome silence. It's technically a no-no to be out of the building, even if the door is only two feet away, but I want a minute to think. And it's not like I snuck out to smoke.

I lean my head back against the rough bricks. Was I wrong to talk about Officer Balboa? I've been successfully avoiding him ever since I posted "The Rumors" episode.

Luckily his pressed uniform stands out in a sea of casual clothes.

Inside, the bell rings. Time to get to class. But when I pull the door handle, it's locked. I should have thought of that. Every school in America now drives all visitors through a gauntlet of buzzers and bulletproof glass. We've already had two active shooter drills.

I walk around to the main entrance and press the silver button next to the door, making sure my face is in the camera's view. Eventually, the school secretary buzzes me in to the front office.

"Do you have a note for missing half a day?" she asks. Out in the hall, the bell rings again. I'm officially late for class.

"I've actually been here all morning. I just stepped outside for a second to get some fresh air. I didn't realize the door would lock behind me."

"Fresh air, huh?" a voice says behind me. It's Office Balboa.

My shoulders tense as I turn around. "Yeah," I say evenly, careful not to meet his eyes. Like prey, I try to stay as still as possible.

He comes closer and takes a theatrical, exaggerated sniff. "Is that a cig I smell? Or"—he attempts a Jamaican accent—"ganja?"

I resist the temptation to roll my eyes. "You can't smell anything because there is nothing to smell." Even as I say the words, I know he'll see them as back talk.

He lifts his chin. "Shouldn't you be in class, young lady?"

"That's where I'm going."

"I'll walk you there." Officer Balboa clamps his hand on my elbow. "We wouldn't want you getting lost along the way."

Once out in the hall, he drops my arm. "You'd better watch your step, Gray. Because I am watching you. You're stirring up trouble where there isn't any. And talking trash about me."

I'm walking so fast I'm nearly running, but he matches me stride for stride.

I speak through gritted teeth. "A girl is dead and no one has been arrested for her murder."

"That's true and it's sad, but it's also old news. In fact, people had moved on. And then you come down here and start it all up again. And for what?"

"Layla deserves justice."

"You don't care about that. All you care about is saying outrageous things to get more podcast listeners."

"Look, I never said your name. I never even used the recording I made of you. And I didn't say anything that wasn't true. You've been married four times, and your new wife went to school here. And you responded to the call about Layla's body being found."

With a muttered curse, Officer Balboa abruptly steps in front of me, forcing me to skid to a stop. His voice is a menace-laden whisper.

"You know what, Gray? You need to stop asking questions. You need to stop running your mouth." Without saying anything else, he stalks past me.

My mind is whirling as I slip into class. Did he have anything to do with Layla's death? Is he the one who keeps sending me anonymous messages, telling me I need to stop?

And if he isn't, who is?

CHAPTER THIRTY-THREE

LIKE IT'S ENTERTAINMENT
Friday, October 9

WHAT'S THE BEST WAY to approach the Trellos? I could mail them a letter or try messaging Cindy on Facebook. But it's harder to say no to someone's face. I decide to head there after school.

As I walk out the double doors, I catch sight of a man across the street. He has a shaved head and sunglasses. A shiver runs down my spine. I think it might be the same man I saw when I was going to Star's. But Firview's a small town. And hundreds of kids go to this school. Even if it's the same guy, there's lots of reasons I might see him twice. Two tall kids cut in front of me, and by the time I look for the man again, he's gone.

The whole time I'm walking to the Trellos', I keep looking over my shoulder, but the man is never one of the people behind me. By the time I get a few blocks from their house, the sidewalk is empty, as is the street. The emptiness is not at all reassuring. If anything happened, there would be no witnesses.

When I climb the cracked concrete steps, my heart is pounding. My knock is far too tentative. I'm raising my hand to knock again when an unsmiling Mrs. Trello opens the door.

I've seen her in photos. But this woman looks as if far more than seventeen years have passed. Deeply etched lines on a pale face. Purple shadows under blue eyes. Graying hair sticking up in weird shocks, like whenever a piece gets in her way, Mrs. Trello just grabs it and cuts it off. She's wearing faded maroon sweatpants and a matching sweatshirt that are both far too big.

"Hello," I say. "I'm Piper Gray. I live in the neighborhood."

Her expression doesn't change. "I know who you are."

And just when I'm ready to bolt back down the stairs, she smiles. The smile transforms her face. I even see traces of Layla in that smile.

"Come in." Mrs. Trello stands to one side and waves me in. "Would you like a cup of tea? Coffee?"

"Uh, no thank you." I follow her to the living room. The sole decoration consists of photos of Layla. Posed portraits hang on the wall. Clustered on every surface are framed casual snapshots. A few show Layla's sister or parents, but mostly it's just Layla at every age from baby to right before she died.

The only photos I have of my mom are on my phone. And I never look at them.

Mrs. Trello sits in a tan recliner with a cup holder. It's the kind I associate with other people's dads. I wonder where Mr. Trello is. The rest of the house feels silent and empty. Like it's been a long time since a stranger has been here.

I sit on the blue-and-tan-plaid couch opposite her.

"After Layla died, we had to change our phone number to avoid the calls from reporters, television shows, movie producers. All the attention was too much, and we wished it would just stop." Mrs. Trello sighs. "Then it did. Now it feels like everyone has forgotten her." She grips the recliner's well-worn arms and leans forward. "Or at least it did, until you started that podcast."

"How did you find out about it?"

"An old friend called me. She thought I would be upset."

I gather my courage. "And are you?"

Her mouth twists. "No one else has been able to figure it out. Maybe you will."

From my backpack, I take out the two mics and the splitter and hook them up to my phone. I clip one mic to the collar of her sweatshirt. Up close, Mrs. Trello smells sour. I set the phone on the coffee table between us, then attach my own mic.

After asking her verbal consent for the tape, I say, "So

Mrs. Trello, what do you think about this podcast? About *Who Killed Layla Trello?*"

"I'm hoping it will make people take another look. The old police chief, Benjamin Bassett, got sick of us bugging him. But he never did anything except grandstand. He liked being in front of a bank of microphones saying what people wanted to hear. That they weren't in any danger, that it must have been some evil stranger who happened to be passing through our safe little community. Someone who stopped in town just long enough to snatch up Layla and dump her body in a spot only a local would know. And we were supposed to believe that."

"You think he was wrong?"

"I think it's true most people weren't in any danger. I mean, the choices were"—Mrs. Trello holds up one finger—"one, it was someone who just killed a random person." She adds a second finger. "Or two, it was a predator looking for any girl who was lost or alone." Another finger. "Or three, it was someone who knew Layla, maybe even a friend."

"What do you think happened?" Part of me is already weighing her words, wondering which will make it into the podcast.

"I think her killer knew Layla. And I think they were at that party. John thought so, too."

"Thought?" I echo, thrown by the past tense.

Her face sags. "Oh, you don't know? My husband, John,

died exactly a year after Layla did. He'd gotten a gun, saying it was for protection. But he used it on himself."

My heart contracts. "Oh no. It must have been so hard for you to go on."

"I wasn't ready to die. Not when Layla's killer was out there. Having a life."

I make myself continue. "Can you start by telling me what it was like when Layla was missing?"

"It was both easier and harder. Easier because you still have some hope. Harder because you imagine the worst. A week after Layla disappeared, John and I went downtown. We handed out fliers with her picture, asked folks if they'd seen her. At two in the morning, we spotted this girl wandering down the street, no shoes on. Drunk and alone. Of course we took her back to her dorm. But what if we hadn't seen her?"

"You probably saved her from something terrible."

"Every day Layla was missing, I wore something of hers. Her clothes, her shoes, her jewelry, even her makeup. How could she be dead if her things were still being used? We left the lights on in the house at night, like they might guide her back home. Kids would drive by, staring in through the open curtains at her bed, her desk, her books. As if it was an exhibit."

"You must have felt so helpless."

"After she was found, I used to drive out there in the middle of the night. The news made it sound like it's out in the wilds someplace, but Gilkey Creek's only about five hundred yards from the parking lot at the Bettinger Butte trail."

"Why did you go?"

She looks down at her empty hands, and then up at me. "I kept hoping the killer might show up there, too. Come look at the things people had left in her memory and feel powerful. Or maybe leave a clue. I'd take my flashlight and read every note, every card, look at every stuffed animal, and try to figure out if it meant anything."

Behind me, I hear the front door open, and then a woman's voice. "Who are you talking to, Mom?"

I turn. It's Aubrey, all grown up, minus the braces and plus an expensive-looking black suit. I see traces of Layla in her, as well as Mrs. Trello.

"Honey, this is Piper Gray. Piper, this is my younger daughter, Aubrey."

Aubrey's eyes narrow. "You're that girl! That stupid girl who started a podcast about my sister without thinking how it would affect her friends and family." Hands on her hips, she turns to her mother. "Mom! Why do you have that microphone clipped to you?"

Mrs. Trello seems smaller. Her voice certainly is. "The podcast could generate some new leads. You know how I feel. I'll talk to anyone who could help."

"Oh yeah, right, like that psychic? All she did was fleece you for thousands."

"I got to talk to Layla again. It was worth it."

Aubrey huffs in frustration. "You know that's not true. You could have spent that money on fixing this place up. Spent it on your grandkids. Spent it on a scholarship in Layla's name. But no, you threw it at some charlatan who wanted to capitalize on your pain." She flings one arm out to point at me. "And now you're showing the same lack of judgment by participating in a trashy podcast where listeners get all revved up about crime like it's entertainment. I wondered when one of them would want to use Layla." She makes a disgusted noise. "But I never thought it would be a kid."

I try to make my voice strong, but it comes out wispy. "Do you really think it's better Layla is forgotten and her killer's free?"

Aubrey draws herself up until she looms over me. "Oh, like you're going to solve it by rehashing years-old news stories. If the police couldn't find the killer back then, some teenager is not going to solve it now. You're just turning our family's tragedy into a commodity." She speaks through gritted teeth. "You've started it all up again. Ripped the scabs off. Turned scars back into bleeding wounds."

"Aubrey, stop!" Mrs. Trello commands. "I'm not healed. Not even close. If Piper can find the answers, then she's got my blessing."

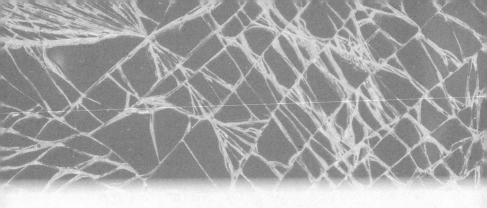

CHAPTER THIRTY-FOUR

PARTIAL TRANSCRIPT OF EPISODE 6 OF *WHO KILLED LAYLA TRELLO?*: "THE FAMILY"

Air date: October 11

I'VE HAD TO ASK myself if it's wrong to bring up these painful memories for Layla Trello's family and friends. Especially since I don't know if I can actually uncover the truth about her murder. I've been told this podcast is making old wounds bleed again. Others, equally close to the story, welcome the attention.

When she died, Layla was one member of a four-person family. A year after Layla's death, her father, John, died. Her sister, Aubrey, did not want to talk about Layla's death. Her mother, Cindy, was eager to share her thoughts.

Cindy: Layla had so much life ahead of her and she was

cheated out of it. She doesn't deserve to have her murder be the only thing people remember about her.

Piper voice-over: While I was visiting Mrs. Trello, she showed me a huge photo album filled with pictures of Layla. Crawling, standing, taking her first steps. By the time she was five or six, she seemed to be in constant motion, resulting in many pictures where part of her is a blur.

Piper: She looks like she was always on the move.

Cindy: It's why she was such a natural at running. I can't help wondering if she ran from her killer. If he tracked her down and shot her. Hunted her like an animal.

Piper: How did you feel when you learned Layla had disappeared?

Cindy: Layla had told us she was going to Star's house, but nothing about the party. When we found out she'd lied to us, John felt guilty. He thought he'd come down on her too hard in the past, grounding her and such. He worried Layla might have wanted to call us that night, but was afraid we'd be mad.

Piper: Your mind must spin with what-ifs.

Cindy: After Layla disappeared, there were so many rumors. That she had run away or left with a married man. Even though I knew she wouldn't do those things, I still secretly hoped one was true. Because if your daughter is alive, there's hope. You can still fix things.

Piper: And then they found Layla's body.

Cindy: When the police came to tell us, I heard myself

screaming. I ran out the front door and didn't stop. You know how busy Tulip Avenue gets. I was thinking I would just throw myself into traffic. Instead I fell on my knees at the intersection, still screaming. John led me back home. The police wouldn't give us her body back for two days. Her body was a crime scene.

Piper voice-over: But as far as we know, no clues were found on Layla's body. It was discovered on a Wednesday and she was laid to rest on Saturday afternoon. Mourners packed Terrace Lutheran Church that day. The pews were so crowded some people had to listen to the service on speakers out in the foyer. The detectives were there, too.

Piper: The police were at the burial as well, right?

Cindy: They were a few hundred yards away. That part was just for immediate family, so it wasn't like there was a big crowd. They told us they would be looking for anyone loitering, maybe wanting to enjoy what had been done to her. Done to us.

Piper: Speaking of the police, what did you think of the school resource officer? Had Layla ever mentioned him? I've heard a rumor that she might have provided him with information about drugs at school.

Cindy: What? That's the first I've heard of it. It doesn't sound like Layla. What it does sound like is one of those rumors people were spreading around.

Piper voice-over: After Layla was buried, the family was mostly on their own. The updates from the police came less and less frequently.

Cindy: At first I couldn't sleep because Layla was missing and I thought she might need me. After they found her body, I couldn't sleep because I'd have nightmares about her being tied to a post in front of a firing squad. Or in my dream, faceless strangers would be laughing and shooting at her while she ran back and forth like one of those duck cutouts in an arcade. For a long time, it was like Layla died a different death every night.

Piper: That must have made it impossible to sleep.

Cindy: After John died, I started spending nights in his recliner, trying to trick myself. Because I have fewer nightmares if I catnap.

Piper: And John suffered, too.

Cindy: He put a letter in Layla's coffin promising he would get justice for her. It just ate him up that he couldn't. Every time he saw someone from Layla's school, he wanted to find out what they knew. I begged for him to stop, and finally the police chief ordered him to. He treated all her friends like they were suspects.

Piper: Did you feel the same way?

Cindy: I didn't think they'd killed her, but no one at the party reported her missing. Not one of her so-called friends. They had plenty of time to hide the kegs, to clean up the mess. Maybe even to hide evidence of my daughter's murder. It was like the most important thing was not narcing rather than finding Layla's killer. I used to beg Danny and Hunter to tell me the truth. The only people who really know what happened that night are the Hitchens brothers. When Layla's body was found, I tried calling their house. Calling their cell phones after Star gave me their numbers. At first they wouldn't answer, and then they blocked my calls.

Piper: Did you ever hear about Layla possibly being involved with Hunter? I've seen an old photo of them where they looked quite close.

Cindy: She did have a little crush on Hunter, but he was Star's boyfriend, and that friendship was more important to her. That was why she was so upset to catch him cheating.

Piper: What do you think happened that night?

Cindy: John and I used to be sure Danny was the killer. But after hearing your podcast, now I'm thinking Hunter must have shot Layla after she confronted him. But the police never looked at either boy seriously. Not when their father was Rich Hitchens.

CHAPTER THIRTY-FIVE

NOT EVEN REAL
Wednesday, October 14

I FEEL READY TO interview Danny Hitchens. But how? I've looked for him on people search sites. While I've found a dozen addresses around Firview for him, none are current.

The podcast has been downloaded nearly four thousand times when I wake up to an e-mail. "If you want to talk to Danny Hitchens, this is where he lives. He works nights and gets home around six thirty in the morning."

During free period, I show the message to Jonas. "I'm going out there before school tomorrow to see if he'll talk to me." School doesn't start until eight forty-five so there should be time.

Jonas straightens up from massaging his leg. He's gotten comfortable enough around me to occasionally unfasten his prosthesis, leaving it in the leg of his sweatpants.

He says the stump needs to breathe. Now he says, "Oh no you're not."

"Excuse me? I need to for the podcast."

"I mean you're not going by yourself. A, you've been doing a podcast that basically accuses this guy of having something to do with a murder. B, that's a sketchy part of town. And C, I'm not letting you go by yourself."

Even though I was secretly hoping for this response, I still make a show of arguing before agreeing.

From outside comes the PE teacher's whistle, as faint as a bird's call. Jonas looks toward the window. "Maybe sometime you should go out there and look at the new stands," he says. "The ones they installed over the summer."

"Why would I want to do that?"

"To look at the plaque thanking the donor."

Understanding dawns. "Is the word *Hitchens* on there?"

He nods. "And he's pretty powerful in this town. You know, Piper, sometimes I think you don't take this seriously enough."

"You're not the only one who thinks like that." I open one of the vaguely threatening e-mails I've gotten while another part of my brain warns me not to.

Jonas softly reads the words from my computer screen. " 'Stop asking questions. What you're doing isn't safe.' " He turns to me. "And you don't think that's ominous?"

"I've gotten a few like that. It's just someone pranking

me," I say with more conviction than I feel. "They're not even real e-mail addresses."

"Of course they're not!" His voice is louder. "You move here and think you can just ask a few questions and get to the bottom of something the police couldn't solve. This isn't one of those murder-mystery dinner plays where everyone stands up and takes a bow afterward. Or a faux reality show where someone is watching just off camera, ready to jump in and save you. A real girl died." His eyes are anguished. "And I don't want another real girl to die." He puts his hand on my forearm.

For a moment, I rest mine on top of his. His voice was loud enough that the librarian has turned to look at us. "I'll be fine." I disengage and scoot back.

When I get home from school, there are two packages from Amazon on the front porch. I use my foot to push them inside as I unlock the door. One of them bears my name, even though I haven't ordered anything.

Feeling a pleasant curiosity, I open it. Inside are two things.

One is a book called *How to Survive the Death of a Child*. The other is a pink-and-white heart-shaped wreath made of artificial carnations and roses. It's a funeral wreath. A pink ribbon cuts across it diagonally.

On the ribbon, a name is printed in white cursive letters.

Piper.

CHAPTER THIRTY-SIX

BACK TO THE BEGINNING

Thursday, October 15

THIS MORNING, THE PLAN is for Jonas to get an Uber and then pick me up before we go to Danny's. Now I peep out into the darkness. I don't see anyone, but that doesn't mean someone isn't watching me.

There was no note in the box. There didn't need to be. The meaning was clear. If I don't stop, I might be just as dead as Layla. I slid the box under my bed and tried to forget it was there.

Because I can't stop now.

On the dining room table is a note for Gretchen and Dad saying I'm going to school early to study. Behind me, the house is quiet and dark.

My phone buzzes. It's Jonas, texting me the license

number, model, and color of the Uber. A minute later, it pulls up to the curb.

I say hi to the middle-aged female driver as I'm getting in the back next to Jonas. He's wearing the porkpie hat from Fair Value. I keep turning to see if anyone is following us, but the street is empty.

Around us, the houses get closer together, the yards less tended. Some of the houses are abandoned, the windows boarded up.

"What do you keep looking at?" Jonas turns and looks at the empty street behind us.

"Nothing," I say.

Eventually the houses are replaced by strip malls and apartment buildings with no green space at all. It turns out that Danny lives in one of five identical buildings.

After the driver drops us off, it takes a bit to find the right block of apartments. No one answers when we knock. We sit down to wait at a beat-up picnic table surrounded by cigarette butts. It has a view of the parking lot.

Jonas, who has been bouncing his good foot, stills as an old white Econoline van pulls into the lot. A guy with stooped shoulders gets out. It's Danny. I recognize his face, but his appearance is still a shock. His sun-streaked hair is now threaded with gray. While he's not overweight, he's dressed in dad jeans and a long-sleeved denim shirt. It's hard to imagine him as a fighter. Danny's focused on finding one of a couple dozen keys on his key ring as he walks toward us.

We get to our feet. I make myself intercept him about ten feet from his door. What should I call him? Danny doesn't seem like the right name for someone nearing forty. Is he Dan now? Or Daniel? Mr. Hitchens? Although he doesn't seem like a mister, either.

In the end, I go back to the beginning. "Danny?" I hold out my hand. "I'm Piper Gray. And this is my friend Jonas Shortridge."

His puffy eyes widen, but not for me. "I know who this guy is. He struck out sixteen against Melton." His mouth twists as he pumps Jonas's hand. "I'm so, so sorry about what happened, man. Especially after you got all those D1 offers." Then he looks back to me. "Why are you guys here?"

So much for thinking everyone is listening to my podcast. "Um, I wanted to talk to you because I started a podcast about something that happened almost twenty years ago."

The life leaves his eyes. "This is about Layla." It isn't a question.

I nod. "I'm trying to figure out what happened that night."

With one thumb, he pushes up his wire-framed glasses. "And you think I know?"

"I just want to get your side of the story."

He sighs and closes his eyes. When he opens them, I'm surprised to hear him say, "Okay." He turns and puts his key into the lock. Jonas and I look at each other. I'm half grinning, thinking, *This is really going to happen*, but Jonas just looks sad. In a way, he and Danny Hitchens have the same problem: yoked to a terrible story about a dead girl.

The door swings open, releasing the stale fug of cigarette smoke. We follow Danny inside. An overflowing ashtray rests on the coffee table, another balances on the arm of the recliner, and a third sits on the Formica table in the dining room nook. The lumpy ashtray on the recliner was clearly made out of clay by some kid, and it's hard to think of anything sadder than that.

He gestures for us to sit, then grabs a pink plastic bowl holding a few Cheerios from the coffee table and puts it in the sink. On the way back, he closes the door to a small bedroom with an unmade bed.

Jonas and I take a seat on the couch. It's squishy, upholstered in blue fabric that reminds me of a nylon tent. Danny takes the recliner angled to face the flat-screen TV, twisting to face us. A few unframed posters hang on the walls. One reads in thick calligraphy, BUT FOR THE GRACE OF GOD. Another says KEEP IT SIMPLE, STUPID. The initial letters are red, spelling out KISS.

Danny sees me looking. Taking a pack of Marlboros from his shirt pocket, he says, "I have an addictive personality." He picks up a plastic lighter from the table and lights the cigarette. "These days, I basically just go to work and NA or AA. Narcotics Anonymous, Alcoholics Anonymous. I'm not picky. Never have been, which has always kinda been my problem. I know every meeting within a twenty-mile radius. I used to just go through the motions. Sometimes they make AA part of probation. But now I'm really a believer. You know, let go and let God." He blows out a perfect smoke ring. "So tell me more about this podcast."

I open my backpack and pull out what I think is my splitter. But it's really my old decommissioned phone, the one my mom bought me. I slide it back, feeling a pinch of longing for her.

"That's cool," Danny says as I plug everything in. "Everything's so little these days."

"Should I call you Mr. Hitchens?" Leaning into the fog of smoke, I quickly clip the mic on his collar.

His smile is more like a wince. "Mr. Hitchens is my dad. Just call me Danny."

I sit back down on the springy couch. It feels like the whole thing is made of foam. After going through the disclaimers, I get Danny to verbally agree to everything. He doesn't seem like a detail person.

He clears his throat. "Sorry, I've gotten a little rusty at talking. Even in meetings, I'm not a big sharer. And working nights, I don't see anybody. I go in and mop the floors, empty the wastebaskets, clean the toilets." He sighs. "I'm thirty-five, and I still work for my dad." He waves his hand. "Don't put that in there, okay?"

"Okay," I echo.

"I never thought I would end up like this, you know? I guess I just didn't think much about what it would be like to be an adult." Danny shakes his head, making his combed-forward bangs fall back, revealing the high expanse of his forehead.

"So what have you done since high school?"

His smile is without a trace of humor. "Mostly gone to rehab on my dad's dime. And to jail a few times. Only now I'm finally clean, and my dad still won't hardly look at me." He brightens. "At least he trusts me enough now to give me the keys to the dealerships. The old Danny might have been tempted, but the new Danny just takes it one day at a time. Like they say, 'You aren't responsible for your disease, but you are responsible for your behavior.' So that's me now. Danny Hitchens. Responsible." His lips twist.

CHAPTER THIRTY-SEVEN

THE SAME RHYTHM
Saturday, October 17

JONAS AND I WORKED on editing the next episode—the one I'm going to call "The Couple"—the last two free periods, but we didn't get very far. He offered to help me over the weekend. With the Sunday night deadline looming, I said yes. Luckily he suggested I come over to his house. If Gretchen has rules about beds being made, I'm sure she would have a lot more rules about having a boy in my room.

Today I'm wearing flared yellow corduroys, a white T-shirt, and an old Pendleton cardigan with leather buttons and orange, yellow, and red stripes across the chest. On the back of the sweater is a brown Native American design.

Jonas lives about ten blocks away, on the other side of

the cemetery. I keep an eye out for the bald man, but I don't see anyone suspicious. The day is cool and bright, and it's hard to believe anyone would really hurt me. Jonas's house is long and low, ranch-style. Next to the three steps to the front porch is a wooden ramp. Jonas told me he was in a wheelchair after the accident, waiting for his stump to heal enough to be fitted for a prosthesis.

I press the doorbell, my stomach doing a little flip. Will it be answered by one of his parents?

But instead, it's Jonas who opens the door, with Fred nosing past his knees, barking in excitement. When I try to go inside, Fred knocks me into Jonas. There's an awkward little dance as he steadies himself on me. Then I step back.

"Yeah, I know," Jonas says, shushing the dog. "You like her."

"I like him, too," I say, scratching Fred behind one floppy yellow ear.

As I glance around the living room, he says, "My dad's at Home Depot and my mom's doing a wedding." The decor looks more random than Dad and Gretchen's. Also more lived-in and comfortable.

"She's a florist?"

"Nondenominational officiant. She does weddings for people who want a ceremony that's spiritual but not religious." He turns toward the hall running off the living room. "My room's down here." After I step inside, he pushes Fred out and closes the door. "Sorry," he says, flushing slightly, "if he stayed in here he would just demand affection."

I survey his room while trying not to look like I'm looking. His bed is made, and I wonder if it is all the time. His room is all white and gray: white walls, gray-and-white duvet cover, white bedside table with a metal articulating lamp. His closet door is open, and inside a pair of silver crutches leans in a corner. Above the bed is a blown-up black-and-white photograph. It shows a baseball pitcher. A second later, I realize it's Jonas, with both his legs and black paint under his eyes.

But it's his podcasting setup that really draws my eye. In one corner, a six-foot-long table sits on top of a gray rug. The walls around it are covered with charcoal-gray acoustic panels. On the table are two mics on stands, both of them much larger and more professional-looking than mine. One has a pop filter in front of it. His laptop sits between a laser printer and two pairs of black over-the-ear headphones.

"I thought if you wanted, you could record your voice-overs here."

"For sure."

Jonas helps me start deciding what to keep and what to discard from our interview with Danny. Together we figure out what order to tell it in and how to pace it.

After a couple of hours, I ask where the bathroom is. When I come back into Jonas's room, I pass a bulletin board near the door that I hadn't noticed earlier. In one corner is a small picture of Jonas and a girl. That must be her. Suzie. The girl that killed a big part of Jonas when she caused the accident that took her life as well.

I don't think I've paused, but I must have.

"When you think about your mom," he says in a low voice, "do you keep going over things in your mind, imagining what you should have said? How you should have acted?"

"Yeah. All the time." I can't make myself say more than that. How many times have I wished I'd told her to stop doing what I'd guessed she was doing? That I had kept her safe, even though she was the one who was supposed to be the adult.

A little while later his dad softly knocks on the door and then comes in with a bowl of chips. I can't tell if he's disappointed or pleased that we are all business.

Even though we are just focused on the work, my body is hyperconscious of Jonas's. Our knees are touching, our breathing has fallen into the same rhythm. I can smell the same slightly spicy scent I noticed when I helped him up the first day I met him. It's not shampoo or Axe or anything artificial. It's just his natural smell.

When I record the voice-overs I look up to find him watching me with a half smile. I look away, feeling self-conscious and oddly happy.

When we're done, I walk home, the whole world feeling different.

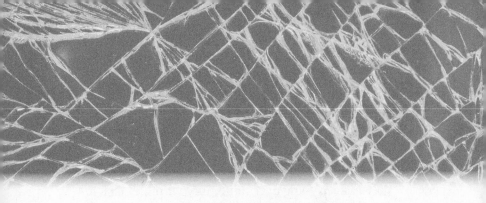

CHAPTER THIRTY-EIGHT

PARTIAL TRANSCRIPT OF EPISODE 7
OF *WHO KILLED LAYLA TRELLO?*:
"THE COUPLE"
Air date: October 18

IN A NEWSPAPER INTERVIEW that took place immediately after Layla died, Danny Hitchens admitted that he wasn't the, quote, greatest guy in the world, end quote, but said Layla loved him anyway.

And it's true that to onlookers the two did seem very much in love. People have told me everyone joked about how Danny and Layla were literally joined at the hip. When they were together, Layla would put her arm around his waist and slide one finger into his belt loop. And Danny would wrap both arms around her, like he was afraid Layla was going somewhere.

What really happened at the party? Danny said she left, Star said Layla was going to confront Hunter, and an unnamed source saw Layla arguing with Hunter on the lawn. Other people who were at the party haven't been able to add anything. Scotty R. told me he spent the last half of the party in a bedroom, throwing up in a wastebasket. Another guy who didn't want me to use his name told me he was in a different bedroom with a girl. Some people I've reached out to don't want to talk to me at all. Some haven't even acknowledged my requests. Others I simply haven't been able to find.

But Danny Hitchens agreed to talk to me. He had a cigarette going the whole time. I don't think it was a sign he was nervous. Or if it was, judging by the already overflowing ashtrays, he's always nervous. I was nervous, too. Was I sitting across from a killer?

But as you'll hear, Danny did answer many of my questions. I should note that a few times throughout the course of this interview, you'll hear the voice of my assistant, Jonas Shortridge.

Piper: Do you think about Layla much?

Danny: All the time. We were so young then. Just babies, even though we didn't think so. But I'm not a kid anymore. I even have kids—can you believe that? Three of them. Two from my first marriage, and one from a girl I met in NA.

Piper voice-over: By NA, Danny means Narcotics Anonymous. His apartment was decorated with sayings from twelve-step programs.

Danny: I've been sober for eight months. That's my longest stretch since middle school.

Piper: Congratulations.

Danny: Thank you.

Piper: People have told me that both you and your brother sold drugs, back in the day.

Danny: You don't beat around the bush, do you? I can say yes, because the statute of limitations has passed. I'm not proud of it, especially now that I can look back and see how much harm it caused. In NA and AA you're supposed to make a list of all the people you've hurt, and then make amends. I've been trying, but I can't even remember a lot of them. I just know I helped screw up their lives. So if any of those folks are listening to this podcast, I'm sincerely sorry.

Piper's voice-over: As Danny alluded to, the statute of limitations for drug trafficking in Oregon is six years. Once those years have passed, you can't be prosecuted. But there is no statute of limitations for murder.

Piper: Did Layla know you used drugs? Sold them?

Danny: She knew about the former. She figured out the latter.

Piper: A source told me Layla was a confidential informant for the DARE officer at school.

Danny: What? What are you talking about?

Piper: So you don't think that's true?

Danny: No. No way. That wasn't like Layla at all.

Piper: My source said the DARE officer never went after you and your brother, because you were untouchable.

Danny: I can't really speak to that. That's all water under the bridge.

Piper: So tell me more about what happened between you and Layla that night.

Danny: Things were actually going pretty good for once. She looked cute and I told her so. I wish that was the last conversation we had, instead of the one we actually did have. We danced, we drank, we talked to people, the two of us made out. Then Layla went to get a refill on her beer. It was pretty late by then. When she came back it was like she was on fire, she was so mad. She said she'd caught Hunter kissing some girl who wasn't Star. But he wasn't the kind of guy to turn down some girl just plopping herself in his lap. What was I supposed to say? Besides, he was my brother. What's it say in the Bible—"Am I my brother's keeper?"

Piper voice-over: Danny's quote here is actually what Cain said to God when he denied killing his brother, Abel.

Piper: Did you see Star at any point that night?

Danny: No. She was home sick.

Piper: I've heard a rumor she might have showed up at the party after Layla called her.

Danny: If she did, I didn't see her. All I know is that Layla called her, talked to me, and then got mad at Hunter.

Piper: And how do you know that?

Danny: Because afterward she came to me and started complaining about Hunter not caring and wanting me to do something. I was like that's Hunter's business, not mine. And then she stormed off. I thought she was still in the house. I didn't realize she'd left until I tried to find her. To be honest, I wasn't sober. So my memory's not so good.

Jonas: If you were drinking, how do you know you didn't have anything to do with what happened to Layla?

Danny: There's no way I would have hurt Layla. Or forgotten I had done it.

Piper: I know you overdosed the morning of Layla's funeral.

Danny: What? No I didn't.

Piper: I read about it in *The Independent*.

Danny: That wasn't me. That was Hunter.

Piper: Hunter? What happened?

Danny: The morning of Layla's funeral, Hunter washed down some pills with a few Coronas.

Piper: Because he couldn't deal with her being dead or the fact that the family didn't want either of you at the funeral?

Danny: Well those things, sure, but we also knew the cops were coming to take us to her. To make us look at her body well before the funeral even started.

Jonas: Why did they do that?

Danny: Maybe they were hoping we would have some kind of come-to-Jesus moment. Hunter was just trying to make it so he didn't care. And by the time they made us look at her, I was wishing I was half as wasted as Hunter. I won't go into what she looked like, but there was a reason her casket was closed. When we got home, he took some more pills. Too many.

Piper: So Hunter overdosed twice? The day of the funeral and then the day he died?

Danny: And I don't think there was a day in between that he was sober.

Piper: Layla's mom is convinced one of you did it.

Danny: Well, it wasn't me....And Hunter swore to me he didn't kill her.

Piper: But...

Danny: We'd always told each other the truth. We were brothers, and that came first. But looking back, I think Hunter might have been lying. Even before her body was found, there were a couple of times when I went into his room and his eyes looked wet. I'd never seen him cry before. And a few times he gave me this weird look when he didn't think I would notice. Just sad, you know? Sad and guilty? Since I've gotten sober, I keep remembering all kinds of things I'd forgotten or maybe just refused to think about.

Piper: A source told me she—they—saw Hunter and Layla arguing on the front lawn.

Danny: What? Really? Because when Layla got mad at him, it was in the house. Oh jeez...

Piper: Do you think he could have done it?

Danny: I don't know. He was my brother. And Layla was my girl. And there I was, in the middle. I used to tell myself it had to have been like the police chief and our dad said, just some guy who happened to be driving by and when he slowed down, Layla asked him for a ride.

Piper: Used to tell yourself? You don't anymore?

Danny: I don't know what to think anymore. The only thing I'm sure about is if that stupid girl hadn't kissed Hunter, then none of the rest would have happened.

Piper voice-over: I left the interview with as many questions as I started with. Danny's family has money. Everyone knows money buys things. Did it buy the police not looking too closely? And how much does Danny really know? Or maybe I should say, How much does Danny let himself know?

CHAPTER THIRTY-NINE

ANYONE CAN LISTEN
Tuesday, October 20

THE FIRST THING I do every morning is grab my phone to check the comments, questions, and tips in my Facebook DMs and e-mail. Every day there are more than the day before. Yesterday there was even an e-mail from a local security company wanting to explore being a sponsor. More and more people are comparing me to Kelley McBain.

Today there's an e-mail from Heather Fairchild, a reporter at the *Firview Times*, saying she's always looking for stories "highlighting the community's youth." She wants to talk to me about my podcast.

I decide two things. One, to suggest we talk after school. And two, that I'd better tell Gretchen and Dad before the article comes out. While I've briefly mentioned my project to Gretchen, I haven't said anything to Dad. So far, no one seems to have brought it up to them, but then again I've got my mom's last name, so it's likely no one has realized we're related.

Once I get to school, I'm stopped twice by other students eager to share their tenuous connection with the podcast. One girl claims her mom's cousin met Layla once, and a guy says his dad bought their latest car from Danny's dad. I slip into Mrs. Wharton's class just as the bell rings.

Mrs. Wharton spends most of class talking about point of view and how it changes the perception of events, but I'm half listening and half obsessing over what my next podcast episode should be about. I've already covered the obvious angles. Jonas's lucky, or maybe just smart. No matter how many games he features, there's always a million more. An unsolved murder offers limited options. Should I discuss in detail the other homicides that occurred within two years and a two-hour drive of Layla's murder, even though none of them seem related? Try again to get the police to talk to me? Paint a fuller picture of the party by using some of the information people have sent me, even though no one has agreed to be interviewed on tape? The weekly cadence is like a giant maw that must be continually fed.

When the bell rings at the end of class, Mrs. Wharton leans in close enough that I can smell the vanilla notes of her perfume.

"It's your fault I stayed up way too late!" she says as the class empties out.

"Sorry?" I let my voice rise at the end, making it clear I don't mean it.

"That was such a good episode with Danny. What are you going to cover next?"

A pit opens in my stomach. "It's starting to feel like all this pressure, you know? Like I have to find some new angle or prove what really happened, and I don't know how to do either of those things."

"Don't all fingers point to Hunter?" She starts to erase the whiteboard. "I mean, maybe this whole thing was already wrapped up before you were even born."

I shrug. "Danny told me he's been rethinking everything. And that he's been remembering more."

"Really?" She pauses. "You didn't tell him about me talking to you, did you? I don't need him showing up here, wanting to reminisce about old times."

I shake my head. "I promised you."

That night at dinner, I manage to squeeze in a few sentences between the two kids. "Um, the *Firview Times* interviewed me today. There's probably going to be an article in the paper tomorrow."

My dad straightens up and gives me his full attention. Even Sequoia and Jasper still. "Why?"

"We have to do a senior passion project. I've started a podcast."

"Oh, really?" He looks interested. "On what?"

"Um," I hesitate, glancing at Sequoia and Jasper, who are staring at me. For once they're not bickering, talking over each other, or insisting Gretchen hasn't divided things fairly. "It's about an unexplained death that happened nearly twenty years ago."

"And this is for the school radio station?" Gretchen asks. "I didn't know they had one."

"No, it's like a real podcast. I mean, it *is* a real podcast." In a singsong voice I say, "Be sure to like, review, and subscribe wherever you usually get your true-crime podcasts." I've said the words in my outro so many times they no longer have meaning.

My dad traces the sides of his mouth with his index finger and thumb. "So anyone can listen to it?"

CHAPTER FORTY

FROM THE *FIRVIEW TIMES*
Published October 21

TEEN PODCASTER CAPTURES WORLDWIDE INTEREST WITH PODCAST ABOUT LOCAL UNSOLVED MURDER

Firview, Ore.—At seventeen, most girls might be thinking about the upcoming homecoming dance. Not local teen Piper Gray. She's become a podcaster with a growing following.

Welcome to the world of podcasts, where a stranger murmurs in your ear while you commute to work, do the laundry, or go for a run.

It's a form of storytelling as old as cavemen gathering around a fire to listen to an exciting tale. The modern twist is it requires an internet connection so that you can listen to it or download it to the device of your choice. But because it's on the internet, that means listeners from all over the world can access it.

"I've had downloads from seven countries and thirty-two states," Gray says proudly.

Podcasts, which have been increasingly popular, have carved out a space next to books, TV shows, movies, and even radio. Radio shares DNA with podcasts, and many radio programs have a longer shelf life as podcasts. One popular podcast subgenre concerns itself with true crime, especially murder. In fact, shows like Kelley McBain's *Dead, Deader, Deadest* make frequent appearances on Apple's Top Ten Podcast list.

Since creating a podcast requires little in the way of equipment, making one seems deceptively simple. All you need is a good story.

But it's hard to find those stories, especially now that everyone is looking for them. What story hasn't been told before?

At the beginning of the school year, Gray, a transfer student, learned about the requirement at North High that all seniors have a passion project. While out for a walk the day before school began, she had noticed the grave of Layla Trello, a former North student whose death shocked this community almost twenty years ago. Trello disappeared from a Halloween party. Twelve days later her body was found on federal forest land with a bullet to the heart. No one has ever been arrested for the killing.

Gray, who says she's a big fan of *Dead, Deader, Deadest*, decided her senior passion project would be to make a podcast about Trello's death.

Trello's mother, Cindy Trello, welcomes the podcast, called simply *Who Killed Layla Trello?* She says it is bringing new attention to the case. "The police chief called me yesterday," she said. "This is the first time in years they've reached out. And it's all thanks to Piper."

CHAPTER FORTY-ONE

TIES THAT BIND US
Wednesday, October 21

AT BREAKFAST, DAD MAKES a big deal of cutting out the article, saying he wants to get it framed. Sequoia and Jasper look at me with wide eyes.

"I listened to it last night," Gretchen says. "Or most of it. I might have fallen asleep."

I wince. "Oh."

"I'm not saying it's boring," she rushes to add. "I'm saying I'm chronically sleep deprived and I made the mistake of closing my eyes."

I nod, a bit mollified.

"I had time to listen through the fourth episode." Dad pulls the napkin from his shirt collar. "I'll try to listen to the rest today. We've lived here eight years, but we've never heard anything about Layla Trello." Getting to his feet, he reaches for his keys in the dish on the sideboard. "I guess by the time we moved here no one was talking about her murder."

At school, all the teachers comment on the newspaper article, and even some of the other kids tell me their parents asked about me. I get compliments on both the podcast and my outfit. Today I'm wearing a top with narrow black and white stripes and pants in a red, black, white, and gray plaid. I've paired them with a black leather jacket that the original owner covered in the most random assortment of patches, including a grinning skull topped with a red candle, the words *Heck Yeah*, a slice of pizza, a Bible, and a huge oval patch touting the merits of Plotts, a breed of dog that hunts bears and boars.

When Jonas sees me walk into the library at the beginning of free period, he takes out his earbuds. "Good article."

I feel a surge of guilt. I was so busy talking about Layla and me that I didn't give Jonas any credit. Out of that guilt springs an easy lie. "I wish she would have put the part when I talked about you in the article."

He shakes his head. "I'm glad she didn't. I don't want to be in the paper. Not anymore."

When I'm in economics class that afternoon, the wall speaker squawks and then instructs me to go to the principal's office. Everyone perks up. There's a few *oohs*, a few curious looks.

When the secretary shows me into his office, Principal Barry says, "We need to talk about your senior project. This so-called podcast. What on earth are you hoping to accomplish with it?"

Stung by "so-called," I stay on my feet. I find some of the words I rehearsed for the reporter. "The goal of my senior project is to raise awareness about Layla Trello's murder. I want to enlighten people about where the case stands and the questions that have been raised." And he has just provided me with an opportunity. "I know you were the vice principal when she died. I'd like to interview you."

He squeezes his eyes closed, then opens them and says, "Please sit down, Piper." He waits until I have taken one of the two visitor's chairs. "I know you're new to Firview and this school. And I know you may not have had the guiding hand you needed before you came here. So you may not fully understand the damage you've caused." He sighs. "When that tragic event happened, I saw it all firsthand. I saw students suffer. I watched this whole community grieve. It took a long time to heal, but we finally did. Now you are undoing all that good work."

I press my sweaty palms against my knees. "But how can you say everyone healed when the crime was never solved? No one was ever arrested for Layla's murder. People are still hurting—her mother, her sister, her friends."

He frowns. "That may be, but what you're doing isn't helping. Wildly pointing fingers in all directions. Dragging

Officer Balboa's name through the mud. You don't under-stand the sense of community that runs deep in this school, this town. The ties that bind us together. Ties that are being frayed by your baseless accusations."

I think of what Jonas told me. And it's clear that play-ing nice is not going to get me an interview. "You mean ties like the new stands donated by Hitchens Auto Group?"

His eyes narrow. "The Hitchens family has always been very generous to this school."

I fold my arms. "So it's not so much about community ties. It's about money."

"Mr. Hitchens called me this morning. He and his fam-ily are understandably upset about your suggestion that one or both of their boys—both of whom graduated from North in good standing, I might add—had a hand in a girl's murder."

"What about freedom of speech?" I counter. "Freedom of the press?"

"I think the questions we must be asking ourselves, Piper, are actually about libel and slander." He steeples his fingers. "I'm not suspending you. I'm not expelling you. I'm just saying you'll have to stop making the podcast and find another senior passion project."

"But it was approved by Ms. Kernow! I've spent weeks on it!"

"Ms. Kernow has graciously agreed to help you find another project."

Principal Barry is practically patting me on the head and telling me to run along. Like he's taking away my toy and wants me to go find another one from an overflowing toy box.

"I'm not going to stop." I feel my lower lip jut out, but I can't help it.

He clenches his jaw. "Maybe I should clarify that I'm not suspending or expelling you *yet*. Because if you insist on continuing down this path, you may leave me no choice."

CHAPTER FORTY-TWO

FOUND IN THE FOREST
Wednesday, October 21

WHEN I GET HOME, I throw myself on my bed. There's no way I'm going to stop my podcast. But how can I create new episodes when I now have to put a ton of work into a different passion project?

I check the DMs for the Who Killed Layla Trello? Facebook page. There are more than a dozen messages. I click on the first one, already feeling a tiny bit better.

"You should be ashamed of yourself, ripping off Kelley McBain!" Guilt twists my gut. It's true *Who Killed Layla Trello?* was deeply inspired by all the hours I've spent listening to *Dead, Deader, Deadest*. Kelley's show has certainly influenced me to make mine. Mine is an homage, though, not a rip-off.

But the other messages are just variations of the first. What are they talking about?

It's been a few weeks since I listened to an episode of *Dead, Deader, Deadest*. When I go to the website, the top part of the page features two things. The first is a familiar photo of Kelley, all lashes and cleavage, playing off the *Triple D* nickname of her show. The second is a link for her latest episode: "Found in the Forest: The Murder of Layla Trello."

Even though I'm breathing open-mouthed, it feels like there's not enough oxygen in my room. When I put in my earbuds and hit play, the feeling only gets worse.

"Today on *Dead, Deader, Deadest*, we look at the mystery of a beautiful teenage girl who disappeared from a Halloween party nearly twenty years ago. Layla Trello's body was found twelve days later in the woods. She had been shot to death."

I hit the pause button, feeling like someone just sucker punched me.

Not just any someone. Kelley McBain.

I start it up again. My head is a balloon that's come untethered. The more I listen, the farther away it floats. Basically the latest episode of *Dead, Deader, Deadest* is a rehash of my series. It's not a word-for-word copy, but it's close. Ideas and theories I pieced together from several documents are presented as Kelley's own thoughts. She doesn't site a single source for the episode. Instead she casually mentions that she learned of the case in a "couple of news articles."

The show's contact page features a dozen links: to sign up for Kelley's fan club, to submit fan art, to buy merch, to submit a case or press inquiry, to book a live event, and to ask a general question. I choose the last one, which opens a new page. At the top is a disclaimer that Kelley is very busy, but a member of her team will try to get back to me.

After I submit the form, pointing out I'm the podcaster who originally brought attention to Layla's story, I google "Kelley McBain plagiarism." The result is pages and pages of links. Some people have accused her of simply reading whole passages from Wikipedia. Other true-crime podcasters with smaller audiences say they've learned not to post podcast transcripts to make it harder for her to rip them off.

I'm still reading through the links when I hear Gretchen come in downstairs with Sequoia and Jasper. Just then my phone rings. The number's not familiar.

"Hello?"

"Is this Piper Gray?"

I instantly recognize the smoky voice, since it's been murmured in my ears for hours and hours. Most recently telling me a story I know inside and out.

But now I'm prepared. I immediately sit in front of my computer where GarageBand is already open, waiting for me. Then I press the speaker button on my phone and start recording.

"Yes, Kelley. It's Piper." My anger bursts out. "The one whose podcast about Layla Trello you stole."

Kelley makes an amused sound. "Actually, Piper, what happened is not really anyone's story. It's a series of facts. Anyone can talk about it."

I suppress the urge to scream. "But I've spent weeks and weeks on my podcast. I'm the one who worked to get Layla's friends and family to trust me. Then you just turn around and use everything I worked so hard for and you don't even credit me. Now people are accusing me of ripping you off when you're the one using all my work!"

I want Kelley to get anxious or angry, but instead she just laughs. She doesn't even try to make it sound genuine. "Talk about the pot and the kettle. Your show sounds exactly like mine. If anyone ripped anyone off, it's you stealing from me. You can't tell me you didn't base your show on my show."

In some ways, we're an echo chamber. I copied her, now she's copying me. Like being in a restroom with mirrors on either side and seeing infinite versions of yourself, repeated smaller and smaller until they disappear.

Kelley is sort of right, but she's also wrong. "But we are different! You're more about entertainment. I'm trying to solve this case. I want to find the killer."

"What are you? Nancy Drew?" Kelley scoffs. "Be realistic," she adds. "How is a podcaster with nothing but a microphone going to solve a murder case when the police, who have real detectives and crime labs and fingerprint experts, haven't been able to?"

"If you don't care if it's solved, then what even is the point of your show?" I'm speaking and listening from two points of view: as me and as a podcaster.

"*Dead, Deader, Deadest* promotes personal safety." Kelley has clearly said these words dozens of times. "My listeners learn about different crimes, how they happened, and what allowed them to occur. It helps them feel more prepared for any dangerous situations they may encounter in the future."

It's my turn to scoff. "Really? Or are you just inviting people to shiver while they imagine what some poor girl's last moments were like?"

"I've never once said I was a journalist. I'm not going out and knocking on doors. I'm not trying to get a scoop. Everything I talk about has already been reported on. I'm not a reporter. I'm a podcast host."

I'm aware of the gulf between us. Kelley's famous. I'm not. She's an adult. I'm still in high school. She has close to a million listeners. Even with all the new interest, I have a tiny fraction of that. Still, I can't hold my tongue.

"That's right. You're not a reporter. Because a reporter would credit her sources. The only thing you really care about is your popularity. Your brand."

"And you don't?" she counters.

I had started recording thinking Kelley would say

something I could use to prove she stole from me, but my words are just bouncing off her. When I'm the one who's gone digging. Who's tried to figure out what really happened. Who was first. But I don't think Kelley McBain's fans will care. There has to be something I can say that will sting, at least a little.

"You know what my parents are? Lawyers. I can't wait to tell them what you did."

But the silence following my statement suddenly feels threatening to me, not her.

"Oh, really," Kelley says. It's not a question. "Both your parents are lawyers. That's interesting."

"Um." Suddenly it feels like I've come to what I thought was the bottom of a staircase and stepped out into the empty air. "Well, my dad and my stepmom are."

"What about your mother, Piper? What about her?"

I hang up.

CHAPTER FORTY-THREE

SUCH TERRIBLE THINGS
Wednesday, October 21

I'M QUIET ALL THROUGH dinner, but after the kids are in bed, I go downstairs and tell my dad and Gretchen everything. About how Principal Barry won't give me credit for my eight weeks of work. About how he wants me to stop podcasting altogether. And about how *Dead, Deader, Deadest* ripped me off.

I'm pacing back and forth in front of the couch. As the words pour out of my mouth, Gretchen sets aside her book, uncurls her long legs, still clad in running tights, and sits up. My dad puts down his iPad.

"Can Principal Barry really do that?" I demand. "What about the First Amendment?"

I sense more than see Gretchen start to roll her eyes. She stops when she sees me noticing.

"People never understand that," she says. "They think it means someone can say whatever they want, wherever they want. The First Amendment only protects you from government interference."

"But that's what makes it tangled." Dad leans forward. "Because the school is the government. So you still have First Amendment rights in school. You can speak out, distribute petitions, and wear clothing that expresses a point of view. But the tricky part is you can't disrupt the functioning of the school."

"What's disruptive?" I ask. "It's not like I started a riot or anything."

He lifts his shoulders in agreement. "That's why it's complicated. Even if the principal thinks your podcast is controversial or in bad taste—that's probably not enough to qualify."

"So I can still do it?" Hope pulses in me. I stop pacing.

"Continuing to do it and getting credit for it are two different things." Dad looks at me over his reading glasses. "The content of your podcast is determined by whom?"

"Me."

"And you aren't making or distributing it on school grounds?"

"No."

"The problem is you fall in a legal gray area. You're not producing this for, say, a student-run radio station. But you are—or were—doing it to satisfy a school requirement."

He turns to Gretchen. "One could argue her advisor gave Piper the authority to make her own content decisions and to operate with editorial independence."

She raises a finger. "But another consideration is who Piper is discussing. It sounds like this podcast has a lot about Richard Hitchens's boys in it. As in Richard Hitchens of Hitchens Auto Group."

"Principal Barry was saying something about libel and slander," I admit. "But I don't even think he knew what that meant. It felt like he was just trying to scare me."

"They're both defamation," Dad says. "Libel is written and slander is spoken." He pushes his glasses on top of his head. "Does your podcast have transcripts?"

"Yes. Which is kind of a bummer, because that's what made it easy for *Dead, Deader, Deadest* to copy me."

"She may have copied you," Dad says, "but again, that's a legal gray area, since you were both talking about the same factual event."

Gretchen shakes her head, looking impatient. "Let's stay focused on your legal risks for now."

"Is defamation a crime?" My voice starts to shake. "Could my podcast actually get me thrown in jail? Or juvie or whatever?"

"Defamation of character is not a crime, but it is a tort." Seeing my confused expression, she adds, "That means it's civil, not criminal. If someone feels their reputation has been damaged, they can sue for damages. Defamation is one of the few areas of law where people will spend more money suing than they can reasonably expect to collect. There's a saying that the last thing you want to see on the other side of a lawsuit is a deep pocket with even deeper emotions."

"It's not like I have any money," I say.

Gretchen crosses her arms. "It could be argued that as a minor in our care, your actions are our responsibility."

Dad says, "Reporting the truth is almost never libel, Piper. But if you made a false accusation, that's different."

"I haven't accused anyone. I'm just raising questions."

He blows air through pursed lips. "Because of his television commercials, Richard Hitchens could be considered a public figure, which makes it harder for him to sue. Courts have ruled public figures have less expectation of privacy."

"I don't even talk about Mr. Hitchens in the podcast, except once Layla's friend Star said both Hitchens boys drove nice cars because of their dad's business. And I mention how much money Mr. Hitchens must have, and how that might have influenced the investigation."

Dad pinches the bridge of his nose. "He may be a public figure, but his sons aren't. One is deceased, correct?"

I nod.

"The dead have no expectation of privacy. The other brother, though, he could sue you." He and Gretchen exchange a glance.

"But Danny agreed to talk to me. In fact, I think he saw it as a way to apologize for what he was like back then." Remembering how *Dead, Deader, Deadest* used some of Danny's quotes word for word from my podcast, I add, "What about Kelley McBain? Can I sue her for using things from *my* podcast in *her* podcast?"

My dad opens his mouth, but it's Gretchen who speaks first.

"Can I just say something, Piper?" she says. It's pretty clear from her tone that a) it's not a question and b) she doesn't think I'll like it. My dad puts a hand on her knee, but she is not deterred. "Why would you want to fill your head with such terrible things? Imagine the families of all these people Kelley McBain talks about. What's it like for them to hear their loved ones' deaths reduced to entertainment?"

CHAPTER FORTY-FOUR

FROM THE *FIRVIEW TIMES*
Published October 23

PODCASTING STUDENT FACES PUSHBACK

Firview, Ore.—Earlier this week, the *Firview Times* featured Piper Gray, the senior at North High who started a podcast about the nearly two-decade-old unsolved murder of seventeen-year-old Layla Trello. Since that article ran, the newspaper has received feedback about both the podcast and its creator.

While Trello's mother has welcomed the renewed attention, there has been a far different reaction about those whom the podcast has mentioned as possible suspects.

Trello's boyfriend, Daniel "Danny" Hitchens, as well as his older brother, Hunter, were both questioned extensively. Less than a year after Trello's murder, Hunter Hitchens died of an accidental drug overdose.

As part of her podcast, Gray interviewed Daniel Hitchens. But according to Richard Hitchens, Daniel and Hunter's father, the younger Hitchens has struggled with mental health issues. Richard Hitchens said, "This outsider took advantage of a troubled young man to parade our family's pain in front of the public."

The podcast also hinted there was some sort of relationship between Trello and a sworn police officer who worked at North High. Although he is not named, it's clear Gray was referring to North's school resource officer, Damien Balboa, who has worked with generations of students in his twenty-three years at the school.

"I've had my eye on Ms. Gray for a while," said Officer Balboa. "I have a nose for trouble. And we certainly don't need a teenage girl inserting herself into an open police investigation just for the drama of it."

Firview police chief Randall Newsome said, "I want to be perfectly clear. Certain people are alleging an officer could have had some involvement in this murder. For the record, that is an absolute falsehood. This is being fabricated by a certain individual in the hopes of driving up podcast ratings. If they have evidence, then let them come forward and tell the authorities. Otherwise they are simply out to damage reputations and destroy careers, all based on pernicious rumors."

Fellow students told us Gray said she used to live in Eugene and claimed she had to move to Firview to live with her father after her mom died.

But after receiving an anonymous tip, we took a look at court records. It turns out Gray's mother is very much alive. She's in jail, awaiting trial for dealing meth.

CHAPTER FORTY-FIVE

THINGS GOT AWAY
Friday, October 23

WHEN I SLIP INTO Mrs. Wharton's class, I shoot a quick glance at Jonas. He leans over, his voice pitched for my ears alone. "We need to talk. I'll see you in the library."

Just like I did back when the school year started two months ago, this morning I walk through the halls with my head down. Even though I'm not meeting anyone's eyes, I can hear the whispers that follow me as I move between classes. I hear the words *mom*, *meth*, and *Kelley McBain*. One guy even yells, "Do you know where I can score, Gray?" and laughs a braying laugh. When my head jerks around, I can't tell who said it. I just meet unfriendly eyes.

Finally, it's free period. I sit down next to Jonas at the table in the back of the library. Unsmiling, he turns and locks his gaze onto mine. When he does, I realize how I've longed for him to look at me with such intensity.

Only not like this. Never like this.

"You told me your mother was dead." His voice is as flat as his eyes.

"I know," I say miserably.

"Why did you lie to me, Piper?"

"I lied to everyone. At least the ones who didn't already know."

There's the faintest crease between his brows. "Who knew?"

"My dad and stepmom, of course. Ms. Kernow. Officer Balboa, I think. Principal Barry. Even those few people are bad enough. They act like I'm damaged goods. Like what happened to my mom broke me, or maybe I was already broken. Do you know how painful that is?"

"Of course I do," he says softly. "You think I'm not damaged goods? Suzie is dead, and I had to relearn how to walk. I'm never going to run the bases again and I certainly won't get a college scholarship for baseball. You think I like being stared at?"

"So, what do you think I should have done?" I throw my hands in the air. "I love my mom. I still love her, even though she did something so stupid. Something so wrong. But if I told the truth about her, first, people would think she was an awful person. They would judge her based on a dumb mistake. And then, second, they would start wondering about me. Do you know how embarrassing it was with all my friends, all our neighbors back in Eugene? She got arrested where we both worked!" My face is getting hot. "And now I see the way my stepmom looks at me, like the apple probably doesn't fall far from the tree. When I tell people my mom's dead, they get uncomfortable, but at least they stop asking questions. If I had said she was in jail, they'd ask why or they'd google her." I put my hand over my eyes. "And when I told you that, I didn't know we would become friends. And then every time you said something about her, it got harder. You of all people should understand. You've never told Alice what really happened with Suzie." I drop my hand.

Jonas shakes his head, making his hair fall in his eyes. He impatiently pushes it back. "That's different. I was trying to spare her. The only person you were sparing was yourself."

"Shouldn't I be allowed to do that? Selling drugs was my mom's choice, not mine, but we're both having to pay for it. I had to leave everything and everyone behind and move down here to live with a bunch of strangers. My old friends have forgotten me. And then somehow my podcast got popular and everyone decided my thrift store clothes were cool. And you know what? It felt like I deserved to have things be good like that. But now people are sending me hate mail because they think I'm ripping off Kelley McBain when it's the other way around. And I'm going to have to drag my mom's reputation behind me like a weight."

"I liked you because I thought you were honest." Jonas sets his jaw. "I thought I could trust you. I told you things I haven't told anyone else. And you sat there and let me believe a lie. Over and over."

"Things got away from me," I say.

Like they have a way of doing. My mom. The podcast. And now Jonas.

CHAPTER FORTY-SIX

YOU KNEW HER WELL ENOUGH

Saturday, October 24

"WHY DID YOU TELL people Heather was dead?" My dad keeps his eyes on the road. He's driving me for my monthly visit to the Eugene jail where my mom's been held since her arrest. We're nearly there, something I both dread and long for.

It's easier to talk in the car. No worries about Sequoia or Jasper popping in. No Gretchen giving me the side-eye. And the freeway gives us a neutral focus point.

"It seemed easier and less embarrassing," I admit. "And it's not like Mom was going to turn up to tell them the truth."

Only now, thanks to the *Firview Times*, everyone knows anyway. My mom sold meth. What did people picture when they read that? Some woman with face tattoos, hollow cheeks, and scabs from scratching at imaginary bugs?

But that was never my mom. I can still see her laughing with customers at the Over Easy, sliding her order pad into the pocket of the pink ruffled apron all of us servers wore, even the guys. "Mom was just trying to make a better life for us."

I'm leaving a few things out. Like how she "loaned" money to her jerk of a boyfriend, Carl. Like how I'm pretty sure Mom had started using as well as selling. About a month before her arrest, when I got up in the middle of the night to go to the bathroom, I found her organizing the cans in the kitchen cupboard by color.

"If Heather had asked," Dad says, "we could always have revisited the child support agreement."

He can't get off the hook that easily. "You should have realized that at some point you were making way more than her. Plus you're the lawyer. Mom might not even have known she could ask."

"That's true," Dad says as he puts on his turn signal to pass a lumbering minivan. "And that's on me. To be honest, I never actually knew her that well."

"You knew her well enough to make a baby with her." Even to my ears, I sound sulky.

Dad pinches his nose, then puts his hand back on the wheel. "Well, when you're young, sometimes you do careless things. We met at this party, and she was beautiful, and we were teenagers, and we weren't thinking." He sighs. "But then again, if we had been, we wouldn't have had you."

"Are you sure I'm not just another mistake?" Tears spark in my eyes.

"Yes, of course I'm sure." He pats my knee.

I choke out the truth. "Mom loved—loves—me. I never really felt a part of your life." The last few months I've felt unmoored, in a strange house in a strange town, surrounded by strangers.

Dad shifts in his seat. "After Heather found out she was pregnant, her parents wanted us to get married, even though we were both underage and we didn't really know each other. My parents put a stop to that. I think Heather was really hurt. She called and said that since I didn't want her, she was going to show me that she could do it all on her own. Show me that she didn't need me to have a good life." He blows air through pursed lips. "I'm sorry I didn't make the effort to see you more. When you were a baby, I was honestly afraid I would drop you and hurt you or something. And with college and then law school, it was easy to make excuses for how I didn't have time. Now with Sequoia and Jasper, I see how much I missed."

When I was growing up, all my mom's friends were like her: young women raising kids by themselves, scraping by as waitresses, house cleaners, or childcare providers. The kind of job where you don't need a high school diploma, never make much money, and sometimes have to decide what you are willing to put up with. My mom left her last waitressing job when the owner got a little too friendly.

She liked working at the Over Easy, but college students, who made up about half the clientele, were not always good tippers. Then in the summer the students all went home and it was down to truckers, who were decent tippers, and old people, who tended to watch their pennies.

To help pay the bills, my mom tried selling Mary Kay cosmetics on the side. When the restaurant's owner got mad at her for talking it up to customers, she had to stop.

Then Carl, a trucker who was her latest boyfriend, suggested an easy way to make extra money. She could offer the other truckers who came in a little something to keep them awake and on the road. He said it was one step up from caffeine pills.

It was meth.

When Mom sold a few dozen pills to an undercover cop, she was arrested on the spot. At the same time, the cops were executing a search warrant on our apartment. That was the reason it was such a mess when I came home from school.

That last day, when I opened my mom's bedroom door, I hadn't found her body, the way I'd feared. Just her mattress crooked on the frame and her clothes tossed back into drawers where they had previously rested in neat piles.

Then behind me, an officer from Child Protective Services had said my name. I'd screamed.

Now I say, "If you had bailed her out, I still could be living with her. You wouldn't even have to bother with me. Instead she has to sit in jail, waiting for trial."

My dad says gently, "And if we put up that money, we wouldn't get it back. If your mom is found guilty, then the court keeps all the bail."

I didn't know that. After a second's hesitation, I blurt out, "But she's not guilty!"

Silence fills the car.

Finally Dad says, "Piper, do you really think that's true?"

I know what the news said. That the cops found hundreds of pills in our apartment. But I don't answer him directly. "And Mom just has a public defender, not a real lawyer. When that's what you guys do. You're lawyers."

Dad exhales heavily. "Come on, you know we're not that kind of lawyer. Heather needed a criminal defense attorney. I still gave her some advice when I had her sign the paperwork to have you live with us. I told her she should try to get a plea deal."

"So if she did, would they let her go?"

"No," he says as he pulls into the parking garage. "But she could maybe get a year plus time served."

CHAPTER FORTY-SEVEN

NO TOUCHING
Saturday, October 24

IN THE JAIL'S PARKING lot, Dad turns off the car. I sit for a second, not really wanting to get out. He'll escort me inside. I'll give him my purse with my phone inside, because you can't bring them in, and he'll go back and wait in the car.

The first time I went to visit my mom, it was weird and confusing. Jails have lots of rules. The guards pat you down to make sure you aren't hiding anything under your clothes. And I could only give my mom a quick hug when I came in and when I left. We couldn't even sit right next to each other.

Part of me wishes I could keep my phone so I could show her photos of Firview, and Jasper and Sequoia, and we could FaceTime with other people, and she could see the outside world.

But then she would notice it was a new phone and I'd have to explain how I broke the one she'd worked so hard to buy me. A phone I still carry in my backpack as a tangible reminder of the sacrifices she made.

Except how did she buy it? Did she use tip money or drug money? Even though it wasn't the latest model, was the cost of buying me a phone one factor in her deciding to do what she did? I had begged and nagged her, saying all my friends had one.

After passing through the metal detector and being patted down, I'm escorted through the hall. Three prison gates later, I'm in a room not unlike North High's cafeteria, with rows of long tables. Two corrections officers sit on a raised platform overlooking the room. In my pocket are quarters for the vending machines.

Finally, my mom is brought in, wearing an orange jumpsuit. She comes over to the table, and we hug, fast and tight. As we do, she smells my hair, my skin. I don't know how much is about missing me, and how much is about missing shampoos and lotions.

When we sit down across from each other, Mom grabs my hand.

"No touching," the guard warns, but I've already pulled away, crossed my arms, and tucked my hands out of sight.

"You're still biting your nails," Mom says. "Is your dad treating you okay?"

"He is," I say.

"And Gretchen?" There's an edge to her voice.

I shrug. "She's nice enough." I look over at the vending machines. "What do you want? I've got like four dollars in quarters."

At least the Doritos, Oreos, and trail mix that I buy give us something to do with our mouths besides talk. My mom doesn't tell me much about her life here. She has said that even though it may look nice on our visits, inside it's not that nice.

I think it looks awful.

As she untwists an Oreo, she says, "I wish you would write more." She scrapes her teeth along the white frosting.

"Sorry. I've been busy." I tell her about the podcast, about how many thousands of listeners I'm up to.

"Wow!" She looks more alive than she has in months. "You could be the next Kelley McBain. Gosh, I miss listening to *Dead, Deader, Deadest*."

My mom has enough on her plate, so I don't tell her about Kelley ripping me off, or my guess that she's the one who told the paper the truth about my mom's arrest. Now Kelley doesn't seem like much of a role model. I don't tell my mom about having to find a new senior passion project or about how Jonas feels betrayed by my lie about her. Instead I just say, "I'll try to write more."

"It would be nice to get mail." She bites her lip. "Carl hasn't been in touch. Not to visit, not to write. Nothing."

I look down at my hands. "In the car, Dad was saying something about how you could get a plea bargain."

Mom closes her eyes. She's not even thirty-five yet, but she looks much older. "To do that, they'd want me to rat out Carl."

"But what about you?" I ask. "I googled it. Selling meth is a Class B felony. You could go to prison for as long as ten years. And you did it because of him."

She puts her head in her hands. Now that her fingers are still, it's clear her nails are just as bitten as mine. "I'll think about it," she finally says.

An hour filled with silences and awkward small talk later, I climb back into my dad's car.

Dad hands me my purse, then starts the engine. When I take my phone out, there's a text on it. Not from Jonas, the way I first hope, but from Danny.

"There's something else I wanted to tell you. Something I remembered about Hunter. Can you come to my place tomorrow?"

Tomorrow is Sunday. "Sure," I text back. I have a debit card with a little money that I can use to get an Uber. "How about three PM?"

"Who're you texting?" Dad asks.

"Just someone from school," I say. Everyone wants me to stop the podcast, but I can't. Not when I'm getting so close. Maybe Danny will finally admit Hunter was the killer and I'll be able to wrap the whole thing up.

Jonas would probably say it's a bad idea to go alone. But he's not talking to me anymore.

CHAPTER FORTY-EIGHT

I KNOW WHO YOU ARE

Sunday, October 25

AFTER SAYING I'M GOING for a walk Sunday afternoon, I call an Uber a few blocks from home. While I'm waiting, I notice there's a voice mail on my phone. I seldom get calls. Not many people even have my phone number. For the caller, instead of a name or a phone number, it just lists "Unknown." My stomach already twisting, I press play.

"Listen up, Piper, or you're going to have to pay the piper." The voice is strange and metallic, run through some computer program that has warped it beyond all recognition. I can't even tell if it's male or female, not even when it half giggles at its own stupid joke. "You need to stop sticking your nose where it doesn't belong. You need to stop your stupid podcast. Let the dead bury the dead."

Starting to shake, I turn in a frantic circle. Is someone

watching me from a car or even a window? Is it the bald man? But I don't see anyone, which makes me feel even more alone and frightened. When the Uber comes, even though it matches the license plate and description Uber messaged me, I almost don't get in. Even the fact that the Hispanic guy knows my name seems like it might be part of an elaborate trap.

Still, I swallow hard and make myself climb in. The driver doesn't talk, just asks if I mind if we listen to music. I say fine and track our progress on the map to make sure he doesn't deviate. But I arrive at Danny's complex without incident.

His van is parked in the same place it was last time. At my knock, the door to his apartment swings inward, even though I didn't even touch the knob.

"Danny?"

I nudge the door with my shoulder just enough to stick my head inside.

"Danny?" I say again, but softer.

The room smells like metal. The curtains are drawn, but the light from the doorway lets me see enough. Lets me see Danny slumped in his recliner.

Or the thing that once was Danny.

Oh God, oh God. Bitterness spreads across my tongue.

Now there's a neat hole in one temple and a not-so-neat hole in the other. His left hand rests in his lap, his fingers slack around a pistol.

On the coffee table is a half-empty bottle of whiskey,

uncapped. Next to it is a piece of white printer paper. Without making a conscious decision, I stutter-step forward, keeping my eyes focused only on that paper, not on the corpse of the man who put it there. Leaning down, I squint at the handful of printed sentences.

"I can't keep lying. It's too hard. Hunter was the brave one. Now I'm finally brave, too. May God forgive us for what we did."

I need to get out of this room. The air is so thick I can't drag it into my lungs. I can't bear to look at him again.

I stagger outside and call 911.

Danny had seemed worn down to the bone, but like bone, he had also seemed strong. But even bones can break.

Is this my fault? Danny wasn't the happiest of guys, but he was genuinely trying to turn things around. Had Danny broken free of always being associated with Layla, of always being suspected of killing her, only to have it start up again when I began my podcast and then *Dead, Deader, Deadest* ripped me off?

Did my podcast tip him over the edge? How much time had elapsed between when I posted the episode about him and when he bought that whiskey?

I tell myself that he'd admitted he thought about Layla all the time. So my podcast can't be responsible for this. Right?

I'm already forgetting exactly what his note said. Something about how Hunter was brave and Danny had lied. But lied about what?

Was he implying he killed Layla? That they both did?

At the sound of a siren, I straighten up.

An hour later, a man wearing a dark suit with a gold badge clipped to his belt approaches me. I'm in the apartment manager's small office, which the police earlier commandeered, and where I've been told to wait.

"I'm Detective Arkell." His head is shaved so close his dark skin gleams.

"I'm Piper Gray."

He ignores my outstretched hand. "I know who you are," he snaps. "You're that kid who's been sticking her nose into the Layla Trello case."

"I'm only trying to find out the truth."

A muscle in his jaw flexes. "Well, one truth is that Danny Hitchens is dead, and now we'll never know what happened to Layla."

I give voice to the thoughts that have been chasing themselves in my head. "He sent me a text saying he had something to tell me. Why would he do that and then kill himself?"

Detective Arkell makes a sound like a laugh. "Frankly, I think he wanted to do three things: to escape from everyone whispering about him again, to come as close to admitting it as he could, and to make you regret what you've done."

CHAPTER FORTY-NINE

FROM THE *FIRVIEW TIMES*

October 27

GUN USED IN SUICIDE BY TRELLO MURDER SUSPECT WAS USED TO COMMIT ORIGINAL CRIME

Firview, Ore.—In a shocking breakthrough in a murder case that has haunted Firview for nearly two decades, the police department announced today that the gun used by Daniel "Danny" Hitchens to die by suicide is the same gun that was used to kill his girlfriend, seventeen-year-old Layla Trello.

While the pair were attending a Halloween party, Trello disappeared after what Hitchens said was an argument. Twelve days later, her body was found near Bettinger Butte. She had a single gunshot wound to the chest. While no one has ever been arrested for her murder, suspicion has long fallen on Daniel Hitchens or his older brother, Hunter.

At the time of Trello's disappearance and death, both Daniel and Hunter Hitchens were questioned extensively. Their father is Richard Hitchens, owner of Southern Oregon's Hitchens Auto Group. Less than a year after Trello's murder, Hunter Hitchens died of an accidental overdose.

The case had gone cold until a local teen, Piper Gray, made it the focus of her true-crime podcast *Who Killed Layla Trello?* In Gray's podcast, Daniel Hitchens admitted there were gaps in his memories of that night but also implied he now suspected his brother had been the killer. Then Kelley McBain, creator of one of the most popular true-crime podcasts, *Dead, Deader, Deadest*, focused an episode on Layla Trello's murder. That episode has already been listened to over six hundred thousand times.

Both podcasts brought renewed attention to the Hitchens brothers' possible relationship to the case. Ten days after being interviewed by Gray for the podcast, Daniel Hitchens shot himself in the head with a .22-caliber pistol. While the contents of his suicide note have not been released, it is known that he asked for forgiveness and linked both himself and his brother to the killing.

At a news conference today, it was announced that ballistics testing shows the pistol Daniel Hitchens used to shoot himself is the same gun that fired the bullet that killed Layla Trello almost twenty years ago.

Firview police chief Randall Newsome released a statement. "While we will never know which Hitchens boy killed Layla Trello or the exact circumstances of her death, I'm still thankful this news might bring an element of closure to her family and friends. And now Firview residents need no longer worry that a killer is still in their midst."

CHAPTER FIFTY

A FITTING END

Thursday, October 29

TODAY, AS I'VE DONE all week, I'm spending lunch period in Mrs. Wharton's room. It's the only place at school where I feel safe from whispers and judgmental looks. I'm just trying to get through one day at a time, the way Danny told me and Jonas. Remembering him saying that makes me feel even more depressed.

Everything's only gotten worse since I found Danny's body. It's not just the police who think I bear some of the blame for his suicide. I've heard the whispers in the halls. I've read the e-mails and the messages.

And even though Jonas sits right next to me every morning in this very classroom, he has not met my eyes once since he learned that I lied about my mom. Now during free period he makes a point of sitting on the opposite side of the library.

My dad and Gretchen want me to see a therapist, but so far I've been resisting. It feels much easier to talk to Mrs. Wharton. I don't have to explain everything to her. She already understands.

"It's funny," I say to her now. "Thinking of Danny has kind of been helping me start to forgive my mom. I mean, Danny was caught up in drugs for years, even though he went to rehab a bunch of times. Talking to him helped me understand how when you're using, it changes you." I take another bite of my sandwich. I've been making my lunch at home so I don't have to go to the cafeteria. "When I first moved here, my dad kept offering to take me to visit my mom, but I'd just say no. I was so ashamed of her. I wanted to hide what happened. Even from myself. But now that everyone knows, I don't need to hide anymore."

"And talking to your mom could help you understand her more," Mrs. Wharton suggests. "Maybe find some closure."

I bite my lip. "It'd be nice to feel like I had closure on even one thing. I just keep thinking about Danny and Layla, reviewing everything he said about her and about himself and about his brother. I always thought I was a pretty good judge of character, but I guess not. I mean, I came away from that interview thinking he couldn't have done it."

Mrs. Wharton spears a bite of her salad. "But like you

said, drugs can make you do things you wouldn't do otherwise. Maybe you were a good judge of Danny's *current* character, but not of what he was like when he was using."

My mouth twists. "But I keep feeling like something's off. Like there's something I missed."

"Missed?" She tilts her head. "You mean because Danny never told you the whole truth about what happened that night?"

"Maybe," I say slowly, trying to put my finger on it. "I keep thinking about the day I found him. It feels like something in that room was wrong."

She puts her fork down and leans forward. "Of course something was wrong. You were in a room with a body. Have you ever been around a dead body before?" She grimaces. "Because I have, and it's really strange. It messes with you."

"When were you around a dead body?" I ask, rousing a little from my introspection and self-pity. It's starting to get boring, even to me.

"Oh." She looks down. "My mom. She died a couple of years ago."

"I'm sorry." It's bad enough having my mom in jail.

"Maybe the reason everything feels unfinished," Mrs. Wharton says, "is because it wasn't. That last episode of the podcast was never meant to be the final one, right?"

"No, it wasn't." I straighten up. "Maybe I need to do one more. To talk about what's happened since the last episode and the questions I still have. Saturday is the anniversary of Layla's death. I could do a live podcast that morning."

Her blue eyes light up. "What if you did it from Bettinger Butte? From the spot where her body was found?"

I feel a burst of energy. "That's a great idea. I haven't been up there yet. It was one of the things I thought about doing but never did."

Mrs. Wharton nods thoughtfully. "That could be a fitting end."

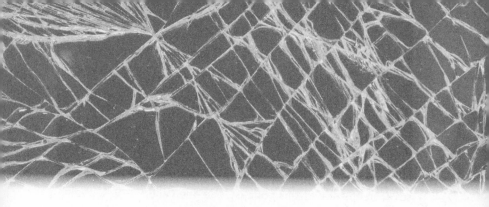

CHAPTER FIFTY-ONE

PARTIAL TRANSCRIPT OF EPISODE 8
OF *WHO KILLED LAYLA TRELLO?*:
"THE DEAD"
Air date: October 31

HELLO, ARMCHAIR DETECTIVES! WELCOME to the final episode of *Who Killed Layla Trello?* Today's episode is called "The Dead." I'm your podcast host, Piper Gray, and today I'm switching things up and podcasting live. On Halloween, no less. Exactly seventeen years ago today, Layla Trello was murdered.

Right now, I'm at the site where everything ended for Layla: Bettinger Butte. Where she went from missing to murdered. It seemed only fitting that I end this series here.

The sky is overcast, the weather chilly, the wind cutting. It's not the kind of day most people would choose to go hiking, which explains why this small parking lot holds only a few cars.

Everything we thought we knew about Layla's case changed after her old boyfriend, Danny Hitchens, died by suicide six days ago. Police have reported that he used the same gun that was used to kill Layla.

As you probably remember, I interviewed Danny for the seventh episode of this podcast, the one called "The Couple." After it aired, he got back in touch with me, claiming he had more he wanted to talk about. But when I went to his apartment, he was dead. In fact, I was the one who found Danny's body next to a suicide note. The police have asked me not to reveal exactly what that note said.

Even though I can't share the contents of the note, I can say that finding Danny dead and then learning he'd used the same gun that killed Layla shook me to my core. Am I in some way responsible for Danny's death? Until I started my podcast, his crime had mostly been forgotten. Should I feel guilty? Or should I feel angry that a killer killed himself rather than face justice?

It's also strange to think of this podcast coming to an end. In the nine weeks I've been working on it, it's become the thing I think about the most. In fact, if you asked the adults around me, it became far too consuming. And now, even though the case has been solved, I keep rereading old articles about Layla's murder, going over the interviews I recorded. For weeks, I've been considering what might have happened, to the exclusion of nearly everything else. How am I supposed to stop?

Ever since I found Danny's body, I've been running through everything he told me, looking for clues. Looking for answers. Trying to make things make sense. I mean, on paper everything does add up. Danny Hitchens, perhaps with the participation of his brother, Hunter, killed Layla Trello. Yet something keeps nagging at me. I just don't know what it is.

I have to confess that I truly liked Danny. Was I just naive? I felt like he was facing his past actions with humility and honesty. Even though he insisted he didn't kill Layla, he also admitted his memory had gaps, due to his drinking. Maybe it was just too hard for him to really look at what he'd done. Too hard to move on from his past.

I guess I'm going to have to move on myself.

But before I do, I've decided to see the place where Layla's body was found. I printed out a map I found online. Gilkey Creek isn't far from here. To get to it, I'm going to go off the trail that leads to Bettinger Butte. It's pretty here—towering evergreens overhead, lush ferns dotting the ground. As I've been talking, I've left the parking lot and the trail and am now going up a little rise. I'm moving through a stand of trees. And there it is below me. Gilkey Creek.

I'm obviously not the first person who's made this pilgrimage. The stream makes a sharp bend, and there, at the top of the bank, a painted white wooden cross has been driven into the dirt. A delicate silver chain with a crucifix has been draped around the cross. Next to it is a green plastic circlet decorated with faded artificial flowers. At the base of the cross is a white china cherub. Its knees are drawn up to its chest and it's weeping into its hands. A small brown teddy bear hugs the bottom of the cross as if trying to climb up. Patches of its fur are missing. It's hard to tell how long this stuff has been here. Some of it clearly for years.

I'm standing on the spot where Layla's body must have been found. Mrs. Trello is right—it's not that far from the parking lot. How hard was it to carry her here? Or did she walk? When did her clothes come off? Before or after she was dead?

Layla was brought into this world surrounded by people who loved her, but she was taken out of it by someone who must have hated her.

And as soon as she died, Layla stopped owning her story. Once she was dead, she couldn't tell anyone what she had been through. Over time, her story has been rewritten a dozen different ways. She was innocent. She brought it on herself. She was careless. She was beautiful. She was a flirt. She was wild. She was helpless.

I'm one of the many who've tried to tell Layla's story. What right did I have to it? As so many people have told me, none.

And—

CHAPTER FIFTY-TWO

I WANT TO LIVE
Saturday, October 31

I'M IN THE MIDDLE of my live podcast when someone shoves me hard from behind. I scream. Arms pinwheeling, I lose my balance and land facedown in the stream.

It's about eighteen inches deep, meaning if I could just get to my feet, I'd be fine.

Only I can't. Because whoever pushed me has jumped on my back. Their knees are on either side of my hips, flattening me out like a starfish. Hands fist my hair, keeping my face pressed below the surface. My mouth is open. I'm screaming underwater, huge bubbles rising past my panicked eyes.

I drag my arms back toward my torso, sliding them over rocks slick with algae, until my elbows are under my shoulders. But when I try to push up to my hands and knees, I can only raise my torso from shoulders to hips, like a mermaid. Still, it's enough that my face is an inch above the water. I take a deep, coughing breath. An oddly familiar scent tickles my nose. Like vanilla.

But then the hands push me under again. There's too much weight on me. I'm dying. Soon there will be a second body in the same place where Layla's was found.

No! Instead of futilely trying to push myself up, I roll to my side, forcing my attacker to shift with me. Now they're next to my back, one leg across my waist, that knee no longer on the ground but pointed up. My face still underwater, my lungs screaming, I pull my knees toward my chest.

They want to kill me. But I want to live even more than they want me to die.

I roll to my knees and then with a superhuman effort, stagger to my feet. My would-be killer clings to my back. One of their arms wraps around my throat while the other hand probes my pocket and comes away with my phone.

And suddenly I'm free. No arm around my neck. No weight on my back.

I turn around just in time to see my phone get smashed on a rock and then tossed in the stream.

It's Mrs. Wharton.

My Creative Writing teacher. My one remaining friend at school.

She's wearing thin black gloves. And she's holding a gun.

"Oops," Mrs. Wharton says flatly. "You accidentally dropped your phone in the water. And when you tried to retrieve it, you slipped and fell. Hit your head. That's one way to end this story. Another is that you killed yourself at the same spot where Layla's body was found. You were obsessed with her. You were so distraught about the podcast ending that you couldn't deal with it."

I take a step toward the bank, but she motions with the gun for me to stay where I am. Water darkens her jeans to the thigh.

Looking at her hand holding the gun, what's been bothering me finally falls into place.

When we interviewed Danny, he smoked one cigarette after another. With his *right* hand. Yet when I found his body, the gun was in his left hand. But why would he shoot himself with his nondominant hand? If you're going to kill yourself with a gunshot to the head, you don't want to miss. Mess up and you could be brain-damaged and scarred.

Unless someone killed him. Shot him and pressed the gun into his hand.

The same person who is trying to kill me now.

"You did it," I say. My voice rasps from the water I almost drowned in. "You killed Layla. You killed Danny."

"And you," she says flatly. "You never ever stop. With your ideas. Your obsessions. Your incessant questions. How long until someone told you that the girl who kissed

Hunter that night wasn't named Jenny? How long until you figured out it was me?"

I blink. "But your name is Virginia."

"Virginia is a lot of name when you're young. So everyone called me Ginny."

Ginny. Jenny. I hadn't listened closely enough. Maybe that's always been my problem.

"So what did happen that night?" I ask. I'm listening to her, but I'm also trying to keep her talking while I make a plan. Any plan. Just as long as it doesn't involve me dying.

"I told you about that outfit I wore to the party. Sexy gangster. It came with a silly-looking silver plastic gun with these obvious molded seams. But I wanted to look badass. Real badass, not plastic badass. My mom kept a gun in her bedside drawer. All black and sleek. It was cool. I mean, it probably had some plastic in it, too, but at least it was a real gun and looked like one. I pushed the little button to drop the clip or whatever it's called. So when I took it to the party there weren't any bullets inside.

"And that's what I showed Layla. We were outside, arguing about me kissing Hunter. Like he wasn't capable of making his own choices. I had the gun in my hand. It felt good there. I'd been posing with it all night. But Layla was telling me to put it away, that it wasn't safe. I turned the gun up so she could see the hole in the bottom where the bullets went." Mrs. Wharton demonstrates, the bottom of the gun coming up next to her face, the barrel pointed to the sky.

No hole this time, though.

"I didn't realize there was still one in the chamber," she continues. "After I brought the gun back down"—she points the gun at me, echoing the move she made seventeen years ago—"I said to Layla, 'Otherwise, it would be bang, you're dead,' and then I pulled the trigger. And it was all over for Layla."

I brace myself for Mrs. Wharton to shoot me, but she just keeps the gun aimed steadily at me. Her face is a mask, but a flicker in her eyes makes me think of the girl she was back then, the girl who had just accidentally killed someone. Ginny, who must have known that in a single careless second she had taken one life and ruined her own.

I realize that many of the stories Mrs. Wharton told me about other people actually belonged to her. Saying she saw Hunter arguing with Layla outside, when it really had been her. Speculating about Star covering up a terrible accident, when in truth Mrs. Wharton was the one who accidentally shot Layla and then panicked.

"What did you do?" I ask. And what am I going to do?

"I waited for people to come running or to hear the sound of sirens. But the music was so loud that no one heard. Finally I went inside and grabbed Hunter. I was freaking out. I told him what had happened and that it was all his fault. After all, he *had* let me kiss him."

The words burst out of me. "His fault! You're the one who shot her."

She shrugs. "Really, it was all Layla's own stupid fault. It was only a couple of kisses. I wasn't taking Hunter away from Star. And even if I was, that just meant she never had him in the first place."

I keep talking, trying to stall. "Why'd you bring her body out here?" Maybe a hiker will come along. Or a mourner, marking the seventeenth anniversary of Layla's death. Today would be a great day for Mrs. Trello to turn up.

"Hunter had a blanket in the back of his car. We rolled her up and put her in the trunk. We took her purse but didn't notice she'd dropped her phone. Hunter started driving, and every time there was a choice, he took the smaller road. By the end it was barely paved. Finally we decided to take her into the woods and leave her body there. Pray that a bear or something would come along. There we were, still drunk, stumbling around in the dark. There's a reason it's called dead weight. When we found the stream, we thought it would take her away. We took off her clothes to make it harder for her to be identified. There wasn't that much blood. Not even an exit wound. On the way home, we wrapped all her stuff in the blanket and put it in a dumpster. I knew my mom would ask questions if I threw away the gun, so once I got home I just put the clip back in and stuck it back in her drawer. Two days later, Hunter traded his car for another one on his dad's lot."

"So Hunter wasn't involved, except to clean up your mess. And Danny had nothing to do with it."

"No." She half smiles, her teeth white and even. "God, it's such a relief to finally tell someone."

There's only one reason she's telling me now. Because Mrs. Wharton thinks I'll never tell anyone else.

CHAPTER FIFTY-THREE

PAIN AND SURPRISE

Saturday, October 31

Mrs. Wharton continues to unburden herself.

"I told Hunter we had to stay away from each other and hope everyone forgot about us kissing at the party." She presses her lips together. "But he was falling apart, drinking too much, taking too many pills." A sigh. "And then one night he crossed a line and couldn't get back."

Did she push Hunter over that line? "And you just went on and lived your life?"

Her brows pull together. "Why not? I really hadn't done anything wrong. Not on purpose."

"Why didn't you just go to the police after you pulled the trigger? After all, you didn't know there was a bullet in the gun. You didn't mean to kill her."

"I still would have gotten in some kind of trouble. And

everyone would have known, would have talked about me. Why should I have to pay for a mistake anyone could have made? When my mom passed away, I got that gun back. I was still afraid to get rid of it in case someone connected the dots." She offers me another smile, her nose wrinkling. "Guess that turned out okay. Because a few days ago, Danny called me. He said he'd been thinking about that party. About how Hunter and I disappeared. He'd thought maybe we'd gone someplace more private, but now he was starting to wonder. Starting to put things together. So I had to nip that in the bud."

The whole time Mrs. Wharton's been talking, I've been examining our surroundings without turning my head. It might look like I'm focused on her, or more specifically, the gun, but in my peripheral vision I'm searching for a place to run, a way to escape, something I can use as a weapon.

And finding nothing.

Mrs. Wharton probably doesn't want to shoot me. Not if she can help it. She wants the story to end with my "accidental" death.

I look past her as if spotting someone. "Jonas!"

And when she whirls around, I run. My heart hammering in my chest, I hurtle through the undergrowth. Just trying to put as much distance between us as I can.

Behind me, I hear her cry out in pain and surprise. It sounds like she tripped. Feeling a spurt of hope, I run faster, heedless of how branches scrape my face, rip at my hair. Slowly, the sounds of pursuit fade. My corduroy pants are so heavy with water that only my belt is holding them up. Even so I have to keep tugging at them. I'm thankful that my black jean jacket covers most of the brighter print of my blouse. Thankful for the shadows cast by the trees, for the overcast day, for the Chucks on my feet that allow me to leap and pivot and sprint. Then I remember the red backpack thumping against my shoulder blades. It's like a target on my back.

Still running, I pull it off. Inside, my fingers feel a familiar rectangle. My old phone. My mom's gift to me. About as useful as a brick.

Or is it? I remember the guy at the Apple Store saying that even a deactivated phone can still call 911. After pulling it out, I shove the backpack deep in some blackberry bushes.

But I'm pretty sure 911 can't track the phone in its current state. So I need to tell the operator where I am.

Still running, I power it on, then risk glancing down. The signal's pretty good. The battery, not so much. There's just 7 percent left. While I'm looking, it blinks to 6. I press 9 on the keypad. I keep switching my gaze between my phone and my surroundings. I press the number 1, hoping I'm circling back to the road.

I don't see the fallen tree branch. The first I know about it is when I go flying. Before I get up, I press the last 1.

The sound of a voice behind me sends a shock of adrenaline from my head to my heels.

"There you are, you stupid girl. Get up."

Oh God, oh God, oh God.

As I slip the phone into my bra to hide it, a tiny, tinny voice drifts up to me. "Nine-one-one, what is your address?"

I can't talk directly to the operator, can't let Mrs. Wharton know I have a phone. But I can say something that will keep the operator listening.

As I get to my feet, I say, "Don't kill me! Please! Don't shoot!" My plea is not a lie. But it's also a clue. A clue that the operator needs to pay close attention. "Don't dump me in Gilkey Creek like you did Layla Trello!"

A flicker crosses Mrs. Wharton's face. Is she wondering why I'm using Layla's full name?

"You're not leaving me much choice, Piper. Now, come on, let's go." She motions with her gun.

"Please, don't shoot me in the back," I beg. "If they find me with a bullet wound they'll know for sure I was murdered."

"Shut up and keep moving!" she barks. I hope her voice is loud enough to carry to the phone. That the signal is strong enough to send it. That the phone still has enough juice.

But even if all those things work, how long will it be before the police show up?

As Mrs. Wharton marches me forward, I pull up my sagging pants again. Only this time one hand closes around the metal buckle of my belt. My body blocks her view of my hand unbuckling it.

It felt like I ran for miles, but in only a few minutes the white cross comes into view. The cross that, if Mrs. Wharton has her way, will soon stand for two deaths.

A slight sound alerts me. I half turn just as she hits me in the temple with a fist-size rock, leaving a wound that could still fit with her story. Hot blood immediately pours down my face, blinding one eye.

But I can see just fine with the other. I've already undone the belt. As I turn toward her, in one motion, I pull it free, catch the tail, wrap it around my wrist, and swing the heavy buckle down at her hand. It strikes her thumb, the metal biting into the flesh. The gun goes flying.

When she scrambles toward it, I punch her in the side of the head with the wide metal bracelet I've pulled over my fist like brass knuckles.

She staggers. Both of us are bruised and bloody, but now I'm the only one with a weapon. I whip the belt at her again, driving her back as I move forward, until finally the gun is between my feet.

That's when I see something behind her.

"Jonas!" I call out.

"Fool me once." Mrs. Wharton doesn't turn. She only has eyes for the gun.

But before she can try anything, Jonas winds up the crutch he's holding like a bat and strikes her head. Hard. If he were still playing baseball, it would have been a home run.

CHAPTER FIFTY-FOUR

SCARS

Tuesday, December 22

I POINT MY FINGER at Jonas. We're in his studio.

Jonas says, "And you've been listening to *Only the Right Left*, the new podcast about what it's like to live life as an amputee. I'm your host, Jonas Shortridge."

I lean into my mic. "And I'm your cohost, Piper Gray."

Principal Barry has agreed to let my participation in Jonas's new podcast count as my senior passion project. He didn't even argue. He's too busy trying to live down the fact that one of his teachers turned out to be a killer.

Jonas was listening to my live broadcast when it abruptly ended with a scream. While a handful of other listeners in various states had called 911 to report something seemed wrong, he alone knew exactly where I was. After grabbing his mom's keys and the only thing he could think to use as a weapon, Jonas had driven straight to me. Later he told me it was the first time he'd driven since his accident. But the need to help me was bigger than his anxiety.

From the parking lot at Bettinger Butte, Jonas heard us fighting. After he hit Mrs. Wharton, I grabbed the gun. The police, alerted by my hints to the 911 operator, arrived a few minutes later.

For trying her best to kill me, Mrs. Wharton's been indicted for assault with a deadly weapon, kidnapping, and attempted murder. She's also been charged with manslaughter for causing Layla's death, with additional charges for concealing her corpse. There's some question as to whether she had any role in Hunter's overdose, but if she did, Mrs. Wharton's not talking. And of course she's been charged with Danny's murder.

Mrs. Wharton left her cell phone at home before going to Danny's apartment, just as she had before driving to Bettinger Butte. That way no pings from her phone would place her at the scene of a crime. Detective Arkell believes she wore gloves to Danny's and brought with her the gun she'd used to kill Layla—as well as a bottle of whiskey, a funnel, and a length of plastic tubing.

His theory is that after letting Mrs. Wharton in, Danny had been lighting a cigarette when she shot him in the temple. Careful not to touch his wounds, she tipped his head back, slipped the tubing down his throat, attached the funnel, and then poured whiskey straight into his stomach.

Before she left, she set out the note that seemed to admit his guilt.

A closer look at all the evidence had put the lie to the "truth" Mrs. Wharton thought she had cleverly constructed.

Not only had she put the gun in Danny's nondominant hand, but there was no powder residue on either hand. And while there was plenty of whiskey in Danny's stomach, blood tests ran after his autopsy showed his blood alcohol content was zero.

But the most damning thing turned out to be the note, the one Danny supposedly wrote. Although black and white, it had been printed by a color printer. Detective Arkell told me that it wasn't widely known, but manufacturers secretly encoded each color printer's serial number on any print it made. The serial number appeared on each page, printing in yellow dots too small to be seen with the naked eye. While originally developed to catch counterfeiters, in this case, connecting those dots led to a killer. Investigators found the printer in Mrs. Wharton's home, as well as the funnel and tubing.

Mrs. Wharton is weighing an offer of a plea bargain—thirty-five years for admitting to two deaths nearly twenty years apart.

As for me, Gretchen started crying when she saw my bandaged head in the hospital, then hugged me fiercely. I've realized that all those times I thought she was giving me the side-eye, she was just trying to figure out how to start some kind of relationship.

My dad's been driving me up every couple of weeks to visit my mom, and it's given me a lot of time to talk with both of them. My mom finally listened to his and Gretchen's advice and took a plea bargain of her own. As part of it, she had to stop protecting Carl. He's going on trial soon. By the time my mom gets out, I'll be a freshman in college. Where, or what I want to major in, I haven't yet decided.

Mr. Hitchens has admitted that he was the one behind the worst of the threats. He had tasked one of his repo men with getting me to stop, and admits the guy went a little too far. Mr. Hitchens had been afraid that the podcast would spur a renewed investigation. All these years, he has secretly believed that one or both of his boys was the killer. Now he knows neither was—but it's not much consolation with both of them dead.

I had the photo of Layla framed. The one that never made it into the yearbook because her hands were blurred. When I gave it to Mrs. Trello, she started crying. I worried I'd done the wrong thing, but then she said thank you over and over. It was like I had returned a tiny piece of her daughter to her.

I produced one more episode of *Who Killed Layla Trello?*, laying out what I know and what I guess. It's been listened to over ten thousand times. Even though it's done, I still like the puzzle of podcasting. And Jonas needed a straight man for his new podcast, someone to ask questions and make observations. On it, we talk about what it's like to move through the world as an amputee, and he shares his tips and tricks for everything from choosing the right pair of pants to finding ways to afford a specialized prosthesis.

Jonas has other limbless guests on his show. Not all of them as the result of traumatic accidents. Some were born that way, or born with arms or legs that had to be amputated. One memorable woman lost most of her arms and legs to meningitis, but still competes in wheelchair fencing at the Paralympics.

Today Jonas has been talking about his new running foot, the kind sometimes called a blade runner or a cheetah foot. It's easier to maneuver in, but when Jonas wears it, there is no hiding he is an amputee. He's decided he's okay with that. And he's also told Alice the truth about Suzie's death.

"Before we close this episode," Jonas says now, "know this. Everyone has scars. Mine just happen to be on the outside."

When he nods at me, I say, "You have reached the end of another episode of *Only the Right Left*. Be sure to like, review, and subscribe wherever you get your podcasts. Until next week, I'm your cohost Piper Gray."

"And I'm your host, Jonas Shortridge. Keep hopping!"

He presses the button to stop the recording. We both

pull down our over-the-ear headphones and smile at each other.

"I like what you said about scars," I say. "I think mine are mostly on the inside."

Without saying anything, he raises his hand and touches my temple. Puts his fingertips right on the scar, mostly hidden by my hair, that marks the spot where Mrs. Wharton bashed me with the rock. And slowly, so slowly I wonder at first if I'm imagining it, he lightly traces the side of my face, moving from my temple to my cheekbone to my jaw.

"A scar just means you were stronger than whatever tried to hurt you," Jonas says.

And then he leans forward and kisses me.

ACKNOWLEDGMENTS

Girl Forgotten took shape during two of the hardest years of my life. Books and writing helped me stay sane.

My editor, Christy Ottaviano, helped shape the book through several rounds of edits to make it the best it could be. This is our fourteenth book together! My agent, Wendy Schmalz, has been by my side for thirty years. They are truly the dream team.

The entire team at Little, Brown Books for Young Readers is awesome, from the strong leadership to the thoughtful planning of marketing, publicity, design, production, sales, and more. Thank you: Leyla Erkan, Marisa Finkelstein, Bill Grace, Emilie Polster, and Jackie Engel.

Megan Tingley, president and publisher of Little, Brown Books for Young Readers, sets the tone from the very top.

Sydney Tillman has wrangled planes, trains, and automobiles, in addition to finding clever ways to get the word out.

Victoria Stapleton, executive director of School & Library marketing, got right to the heart of why I write, and Christie Michel, School & Library marketing manager, has kept all the details straight.

Sammy Yuen designed the beautiful cover.

Ashley Smith, the creator of the *Washed Away* podcast (washedawaypodcast.com), which covers cold cases in Washington State, was so helpful! She explained how she creates her podcast and even gave me advice on what software and hardware Piper might use.

Teen Jay Paulsen, who uses a prosthetic leg, patiently answered my questions about what it feels like and when you might use different types of prosthetics.

Becca Fowler, a 911 operator, fine-tuned what could and could not happen when calling 911.

So many people helped me pull this book together. Any errors are my own.